THE TAINTED

Dominion of Ash

By Frost Kay

The Tainted
Copyright © 2018 by Frost Kay.
First Edition

TABLE OF CONTENTS

PROLOGUE

People were beasts underneath the surface.

Take away their ability to reason and they were as feral as any creature roaming the Earth in search of prey. Hazel knew this for a fact and had seen men turn to monsters, and yet, she never saw it coming.

Her death.

CHAPTER ONE

The End

The world ended in 2126.

Prior to that time, the world was divided in many directions. People preached equality and love, and yet, nobody practiced it. Not really. Every country, every nation, every race, every tribe was broken. Families split apart because of differences of opinion they couldn't resolve. Hatred spread everywhere.

But mankind wasn't only killing each other; they were slowly killing the Earth and abusing its resources. As each year passed, the available resources for human survival dwindled to almost nothing.

Tensions among people and nations rose to an all-time high. Shootings, bombings, crime, malnutrition, and death ran rampant across the world. The U.S. estimated that in a handful of years, there wouldn't be enough resources to support a quarter of the world's population. They knew what this would lead to—war.

Nuclear warfare was not an option. They couldn't risk ruining what was left of the resources. To combat threats other countries posed, the government tasked the biological warfare laboratories to create a solution.

In the year 2020, they founded a lab in the deserts of Nevada and handpicked a team of scientists to work on the project. Their primary objective was to create a weapon that would deteriorate human DNA. In 2025, they succeeded in creating a weapon that did just that.

At first, it appeared to work as expected. The test subjects' DNA would be damaged, and the ability to replace cells would be compromised, causing them to die. It was a painful, bloody death, but in the face of global destruction, some things had to be sacrificed for the better good, or so the government told their scientists. Moral guidelines fell by the wayside.

Next came the antivirus. There was no way to keep

the virus from attacking its own people once it was released, so they had to be proactive. They disguised the antivirus as common flu vaccinations in the prior years leading up to WWIII and added it to the list of immunizations children were required to get when starting school.

When WWIII did finally break out, the depravity and devastation were on a scale that made past wars look like nothing. Deadly viruses were released on the public, each more insidious than the last. But no one had prepared for the super-virus the Nevada bioweapon laboratory had created.

When they finally released the virus, leaders around the world told civilians to prepare for the worst, each hoping that their countries would be passed over.

Alliances crumbled, governments fractured, countries lost communication, and entire cities crumbled from riots and rebellions. In the end, there were little pockets of humanity left that formed communities, but even those were unsafe at best.

The human race became an endangered species.

The US thought they'd won, that they'd accomplished what none else had. They didn't plan on the virus mutating. Their scientists had warned them there were risks when consorting with viruses. They weren't easy to control, and they had a nasty habit of changing.

Reports started flooding in of inoculated citizens dying. There were accounts of people changing in fantastical ways that boggled scientific minds.

Scientists scrambled to figure out what went wrong. They acquired a sample of the new virus, and what they found was beyond anything they could comprehend. Survivors of the virus exhibited traits that would change the course of humanity. The mutated virus no longer attacked the DNA of an inoculated person but mutated the DNA. Suddenly, being inoculated didn't mean you survived. It meant you changed. A large portion of the United States' population died in the first year, because their body rejected the change.

This both shocked and awed the scientists. They scrambled to create something, anything, to counteract the new virus, but nothing worked. The world fell into chaos and eventually darkness.

This is the story that has been passed down from generation to generation. Over time, the virus seemed to die out, or maybe there weren't any more victims to claim. Either way, the world was a dangerous new place filled with monsters and creatures that no one could understand.

A new battle then began. The Tainted against the Untouched. Monsters versus humans. It was bloody and fostered deep-seated fear and prejudice.

It was the true end of humanity.

CHAPTER TWO

Hazel

Hazel dug her spade into the ground and scowled at the weed that refused to budge. Stars above, she hated weeding.

She'd wash dirty clothes and scrub every filthy toilet in the compound before she'd choose to weed, but being outside Harbor's massive steel walls made it tolerable—barely. She brushed her damp hair from her face and sat back on her heels, her back screaming. She eyed the emerald carrot tops bursting from the red soil and sighed. There were worse lots in life. Her gaze passed over the secondary barbed-wire-topped fence that protected the farm from the rocky hills that surrounded their little valley. She could be living out there, running for her life from the bloodthirsty Tainted.

She shivered despite the oppressive heat and glanced down at her dirt-caked nails. Things could definitely be worse. Hazel picked up a piece of her sweaty white-blond hair and inspected the sad lock. What she wouldn't give for a proper bath. This spring and summer had been brutal, the worst in all of Harbor's history. Lack of rain had caused many of the streams that wound through their land to dry up, which meant water rations were being cut.

Dropping her hair, she stared just past the southern fence at the tree line, to where a brook hid in the copse of the trees. She'd discovered it on one of her nightly walks in the garden. Her father hated that she took walks so close to curfew, and sometimes after it, but he allowed it. She didn't ask for much from him except a little peace and quiet from the whispers and rumors that seemed to follow her everywhere she went. Truth be told, she was sure he was a little jealous when she'd escape the madness that always seemed to be brewing in their household. Four older brothers meant there was never a dull moment.

She waved at Micah, the guard patrolling the fence

in the distance. He stared at her but didn't wave back. Hazel kept the smile on her face despite how brittle it felt. She wasn't sure if it was because he took his duty so seriously or because he didn't notice her. But deep down, she knew the truth. The only time someone noticed her was when they criticized or mocked her. She shook her head; there was nothing for it. She just had to double down and do the best possible with what was given her.

Hazel took a swig from the canteen at her hip, lukewarm water coating her dry throat. Lukewarm water was the worst, but she was thankful she had any water in the first place. She frowned at her canteen as she capped it, water once again on her mind. It would've been brilliant if they could have diverted the stream from the forest to flood the crops, but infection was still too much of a risk. The airborne virus had died out over a hundred years ago, but not before it had mutated most human and animal life. No one could be sure what was safe these days. The water had to be run through a filtration system before it could be used and that took time. Not to mention the workers and guards they'd have to send outside the perimeter to divert the stream. It would put a lot of people at risk. She thought it would be worth it for water, but her papa said they weren't that desperate. Yet.

She closed her eyes and imagined, for what seemed like the millionth time, what it would look like. The water would be a clear, crisp blue that flowed over red sandstone, with round smooth pebbles at the edge. A smile pulled up the corners of her mouth. One day, she'd see it—that's if her papa ever let her leave the compound. That wiped the smile from her face. He'd always been overprotective, but it had only gotten worse after Mama's death. She didn't fault him for wanting to protect his only daughter. He loved her, but it made things with the others ... difficult.

A breeze blew gently, and she grimaced as the scent of wet dirt filled her nose. She didn't mind the smell so much as the hot air threatening to choke her. It was comical really; one would think a breeze would offset the heat beating down on her, but it made the heat worse. It was like having a heater blowing in her face.

She lifted her shirt and wiped the sweat from her brow, then rubbed at the heated skin of her arms that looked a little pink. Time for more sunscreen. Unconsciously, her gaze wandered back to the forest edge just past the fence as she brushed her hands along her arms. She'd kill to go swimming right now.

"Daydreaming again, Hazel?" a female voice sneered.

Just the sound of Genevieve's voice made her cringe. She dropped her eyes to her lap and picked up her small spade. Maybe if she ignored her, the hateful girl would leave her alone. She dug her spade into the ground and frowned when she heard footsteps approaching.

Here we go.

"Too good to answer me?" Genevieve asked.

"Darn," she grumbled under her breath. The girl wouldn't go away until Hazel acknowledged her. "I'm not ignoring you. I'm just tired. It's been a long day, and it's bloody hot," she said, glancing up.

The brunette beauty tossed her head and Hazel squinted at her shiny hair. How did she keep it so clean? Did she never sweat? No, she probably *glistened*. She fought a scowl. The girl always looked perfect. Hazel didn't remember a time when Gen didn't look like every male's dream girl.

She brushed another loose piece of white-blond hair out of her face and grimaced as her gritty fingers brushed across her forehead. Great. She probably had dirt smeared all over her face. Hazel blinked when she realized Genevieve was still speaking.

"Have you no dignity?"

She blinked at Gen and glanced around the acres of crops. "What does dignity have to do with weeding? I'm just doing my job like everyone else."

"You're the founder's daughter and yet, here you are playing around in the dirt instead of helping our people like they deserve."

Hazel rolled her eyes and began digging the weeds out from around the carrots. "Sure thing."

Gen's insults weren't anything she hadn't heard before. Everything she did wasn't good enough for someone, but she prided herself on her hard work. She was another cog in the machine that helped them survive their volatile new world. Someone had to do the weeding and herb collecting. Her job was just as important as those who guarded the fence from the Tainted. Without weeding, some crops would fail, and without herb collecting, their people would suffer from all the ailments that plagued them.

"You're alienating yourself and it's not doing you any favors. Despite what you tell yourself, there is a hierarchy here, and you're about to topple from the top, founder's daughter or no."

She ignored Gen. She hadn't alienated herself. The

people had done that once her mama died and her papa began to shelter her. But he wasn't protecting her, he was hobbling her. By hiding her away and excluding her from Harbor's mandatory wilds protection detail, he'd made it even more difficult for her to win the respect of the people.

"Are you done, Gen?" she asked as she yanked another spiny weed from the ground. The stupid thing bit into her hand. She hissed and dropped the pointy intruder, then examined the little drops of blood welling on her fingers. Damn, she needed gloves.

"Did you even hear a word I said?" Gen said.

"What?" Hazel asked, pulling her attention from her abused hand. "Did you say something else?"

Genevieve's fawn gaze narrowed. "Jake sent me to remind you that blending rehearsal is in a few hours."

Right. The blending. If only she could push it back one more year...

Gen smirked. "Wouldn't it be embarrassing if you didn't receive any offers?"

She snorted and wiped her bloody hand on her jeans. Someone would choose her. Three had already approached her father, not that she cared for them.

"I don't think I have to worry about that."

"And why not?"

"Because everyone wants power. Our history is proof of that, and to that effect, I represent power." Hazel jabbed her spade into the ground again. "I have offers, but only because of what they hope to gain by marrying me."

Silence greeted her statement. She glanced up at Gen, who'd crossed her arms, looking like she'd bitten into a sour apple.

"It's too bad you won't have a love match like your mother." With that parting remark, Genevieve turned on her heel and strode away, her dark hair swishing behind her.

The breath Hazel had been holding rushed out. Most days she could ignore the taunts, but Gen's dig about her mother cut deep. Hazel had known what her future held for a long time, and it looked nothing like what her father and mother had shared. She and Matt had planned on marrying when it came time for their own blending ceremony. His death removed all her hopes for a marriage based on love. Now, she harbored hope of marrying someone tolerable who would give her children to love and dote upon.

She blinked back her tears and cursed herself for letting Gen get to her. Marriage was a necessity of life, nothing more, nothing less. But even as she chanted those words inside her mind, she swore she felt a noose tightening around her neck.

Her gaze darted back over the cornfields and to the tree line past the fence. What she wouldn't do to just have a moment of freedom, to be truly alone. A fanciful thought to be sure. The wilds weren't some fantasy world filled with magic and wonder. All that waited outside the wall were monsters, disease, and death. She would never forget the stories her brothers told of the monsters that walked like men, so distorted that they didn't look human.

She shivered despite the heat, rubbing at the goosebumps on her arms, and twisted to gaze at the surrounding farmland. Only once had the Tainted managed to break through their perimeter, long before her time. Now, only little creatures made it past the fence, but no less dangerous. One bite and you were infected.

She threw off the morbid thoughts. Dealing with the little beasties was almost a daily occurrence for her. There was no need to freak herself out over something that wouldn't happen. She eyed the carrot tops and sighed. One row down … a million more to go. But if she hurried, she could finish up the next row and pop by Mesa's for a snack before rehearsal. Hazel grinned as she yanked another weed out. Maybe she'd have pastries hidden somewhere.

Late.

She was late.

Hazel snatched her spade from the ground and shoved it into the back pocket of her jeans. She jogged down the rows of vegetation and sprinted for the southern doors.

"Running late, Hazel?" Old Joss called from on top of the wall.

"I lost track of the time," she shouted, not slowing down. "The carrots can't weed themselves."

"That they cannot. Get a move on, girl."

"Yes sir," she called over her shoulder with a smile. Old Joss and his wife were two of the few that treated her with kindness. They were kindred spirits of a sort.

Disapproving looks were cast her way as she sprinted through the square toward the amphitheater. The doors to the amphitheater sat wide open, as were all the windows. She slowed and jogged up the steps into the dim room. She grimaced. Everyone had arrived already. Excitement over the blending had been abuzz in Harbor for weeks. No one wanted to miss the yearly chance to get married.

Ice seeped into her veins. By this time tomorrow, she'd be married to a virtual stranger who she had to lead the community with. A lump formed in her throat, but she swallowed it down. "I miss you, Matt," she whispered to herself.

She blew out a breath and smoothed her dirty hands down her shirt. Now was not the time to lose it. Hazel carefully edged around the room and crept through the aisles to where Mesa and Baz sat. She sank into the chair next to Mesa and breathed a sigh of relief when she only earned a few glares.

"Where have you been?" Mesa whispered underneath her breath.

"Weeding."

Mesa's aqua eyes glanced in her direction. "That explains the red nose. How many times did you put sunscreen on today?"

Hazel smiled and leaned her cheek against Mesa's shoulder. "An hour ago, *Mother*."

Her friend flicked her on the nose. She rubbed at her stinging skin and glared up at her. "Not cool."

"Neither is being late for blending rehearsal," Baz grumbled next to her.

She leaned forward and gave him an apologetic look. "I'm sorry. I lost track of time."

He rolled his hazel eyes that were browner than green and flashed her a smile full of white teeth. "Only you would lose track of time for the blending."

"It's not like it's today," she whispered. "It's rehearsal. I don't understand why we need to practice anyway. We all know what to do. You stand when your name is called, and you accept or you don't. It's simple."

"Only you would simplify a massive wedding ceremony to one sentence." Baz pushed his tawny hair from his face and reached out to tug on her ponytail. "Have you decided yet?"

Hazel's stomach rolled. "No," she said, trying to ignore the looks of sympathy the childhood sweethearts were throwing her way. They knew this day would be hard for her.

"We miss him, too," Mesa said, slipping her hand into Hazel's. "I still can't believe Matt's gone."

"He only had two weeks left," Hazel whispered, the cement floor blurring as heat filled her eyes. She promised herself she wouldn't cry. "Two weeks, and then he'd have been free." She blew out a breath. "Two weeks left of his protection detail. Life is downright vengeful."

"He loved you, you know…" Baz said, reaching his

hand behind Mesa to clasp the back of Hazel's neck.

She smiled, blinking back her tears. "I know. He was one of the few to notice me. We were never in love like you two, but we loved each other fiercely. He was my best friend, and I would have done anything for him. He was my family." Both had lost parents. They dreamed of making their own family. "Matt would have made a wonderful leader, and father."

Baz squeezed the back of her neck gently. "That he would have."

"If he was here, he'd have been clowning around making everyone laugh," Mesa murmured, a soft smile on her face. "His laugh was infectious."

Hazel grinned despite the sorrow in her heart. "He could charm the pants off of almost anyone. It was practically criminal we were friends."

Mesa rolled her eyes. "Yeah, I remember. He'd distract someone while you'd filch goodies."

She shrugged, feeling a little lighter. "I was invisible. I was the perfect sneak."

"Until you felt so guilty that you'd have to tell on yourself," Baz teased.

She sniggered. "I couldn't help it."

"Baz, would you pipe down?" James, the balding blending proprietor snapped from the stage up front.

Mesa stifled a giggle.

"Sure thing," Baz said. "I'm just so excited to marry this girl tomorrow."

James's thin lips twitched. That was as much of a smile as he could produce, apparently. "I'm sure," he said dryly, before he continued on droning instructions.

Baz playfully glared at Mesa and her. "Why am I the one who gets in trouble for McGiggles over there?"

Hazel shrugged. "It's a blessing and a curse. You should try being invisible sometime."

Both of her friends sobered.

"You've never been invisible to us," Baz said.

"Never," Mesa reiterated. "But sometimes I think you encourage it."

"Why wouldn't I? Every time I'm the center of attention, it's because I'm the butt end of a joke or a sneer."

Baz and Mesa knew it was the truth. She never served the mandatory detail like everyone else. Sure, she served as a helper to the doctor, but that was inside the walls.

"He didn't do you any favors by keeping you inside," Mesa muttered.

"Don't I know it," Hazel said.

"What are you going to do?" Baz asked.

"What?" she asked.

"Tomorrow."

Queasiness assaulted her. She didn't need to ask what he meant. The blending. She'd have to make a choice. A choice that was permanent. When they said their vows, it was '*til death do us part*. Divorce was a thing of the past. "I don't know. I have a lot of thinking to do tonight."

"Who has approached you?" Mesa prodded.

"Jessy, Colton, Aaron."

Baz snorted. "You're not marrying Jessy. He's a total tool."

"They're all tools. We all know why they offered for me."

"Because you're smart, kind, and beautiful?" Mesa supplied.

"Un huh," Hazel muttered.

"Are those your only choices?"

She glanced at Baz, feeling the weight of the world on her shoulders. "They're the only viable ones. Colton and Aaron are smart and courageous, from what my brothers say, but..." She snuck a glance at Colton, who had his arms thrown around two girls, and then to Aaron, who sat stoically down the row from him. Neither boy seemed right, and boys they were.

"But you're the heir," Mesa argued.

"The line continues through the female, but our leaders have always ruled by pairs. It's what makes our community so successful. We need the advantage of both sexes." She blew out a breath. "Now, I just have to pick someone that will be best for everyone."

"No pressure or anything," Baz retorted.

"And what about what's best for you?" Mesa said softly.

She forced a smile to her face. "What's best for Harbor is best for me."

Baz and Mesa didn't believe her. She could tell from the looks on their faces.

Hell, she didn't believe it herself.

CHAPTER THREE

Hazel

She rolled her neck and jogged toward home.

Holy bananas, the rehearsal was dull. James had droned on for another hour before they practiced walking. Bloody *walking*. It was ridiculous.

Hazel veered to the left and right, avoiding people, her faded boots kicking up red dirt behind her. The only interesting thing to happen was when Baz pulled her aside and handed her a letter. Curiosity tugged at her. What was in it? He'd made her promise to open it later when she was home with her family. That didn't bode well.

She skirted around Mrs. Millian's small but sturdy

house and smiled in relief when her home came into sight. It was a medium-sized home that had once been white but was now a pinkish hue because of the sand and dirt. She grinned as a memory from school surfaced in her mind. At the age of five, she'd been shocked to find out that dirt and rocks weren't only red. When she'd told her mama, she'd laughed. The next scavenger trip she went on, she brought Hazel a rainbow of colored rocks and a plastic bottle filled with different-colored soils.

Hazel smiled at the memory and focused on her home. She slowed and walked up the steps to the covered porch that wrapped around the whole place, hosting small tables and chairs to relax in.

She inhaled deeply, contentment filling her. She loved being home.

Brent's voice boomed from inside, "Is that you, Haze?"

"Yeah," she yelled back.

"It's your turn to make dinner tonight, and I'm starving."

Hazel yanked open the screen door, grinning. Her brothers were always starving, even if they had just eaten. The first floor was one giant room divided by a staircase in the center. She retied her hair into a bun while staring at their living room to the right. It held an old brown leather couch and two sturdy wooden chairs her brothers had made. A faded but clean rug decorated the worn wood floor in front of the fireplace. She eyed the socked feet propped up on the couch arm.

She tiptoed closer and slapped them. "No feet on the furniture."

Brent sat up, scowling, his hair sticking up in every direction. "Hey, now. Don't be like that."

"You know the rules," she retorted, cocking a hip. Hazel tossed him a saucy smile. "You weren't raised in a barn."

"Well … if you want to get technical, barn wood was used to repair this house, so…"

She rolled her eyes and leaned over the couch arm to plop a kiss on his cheek. "Always so contrary. How does spaghetti sound?"

"Positively delicious." He licked his lips for emphasis.

Hazel pretended to gag and rounded the stair, entering the kitchen. "Could you light the woodstove in here?"

Brent groaned. "It's too damn hot to light that."

"Then start a fire in the pit and I'll cook outside tonight," she called while poking around their cabinets for some of her canned tomatoes.

"Will do, sis."

She shook her head as boots tromped across the wooden floor; the screen slapped closed, signaling Brent's departure. He walked everywhere with boot-stomping purpose. He was about a subtle as a gun.

Matt had been like that, too.

The thought stopped her in her tracks. Hazel rubbed at her chest where the ache began. Tomorrow would be so hard without him. She placed both hands on the dark wooden countertop and tried to breathe through her heartache. Matt seemed to haunt her every step these last few days. It seemed odd that all their plans turned to ash in just one moment. Their entire future disappeared in an instant, and in its place was a frightening new one. One that required her to marry a stranger.

"What am I to do, Matty?" she whispered, squeezing her eyes closed.

She didn't have much more time to decide. Hazel exhaled and opened her eyes. Her decision needed to be made tonight. No sense in fretting about it now. She'd talk it over with Papa when he got home. He'd help her make the right decision. Shakily, she straightened and moved to the next cabinet. Deep red peeking out from between last year's canned carrots caught her eye.

"There you are."

She pushed the carrots aside and reached up, wrapping her fingers around a jar of tomatoes when hands skated up her sides, tickling her ribs. Hazel screeched and leapt in the air, spinning. Her brother Joseph stood smirking behind her, his light green eyes dancing with mirth.

"A little jumpy, sis?"

"You little devil," Hazel growled, her fingers squeezing the glass filled with tomatoey goodness until they turned white. "I could have dropped the tomatoes!"

He eyed her clenched fingers. "I doubt you would have dropped them if the color of your fingers is anything to go by. Plus, I would have caught them if you had. I'm practically a ninja these days."

Her eyes narrowed. "How do *you* know what ninjas are?"

"I read about them in a book once. They were renowned for their fighting skills and battle prowess." He puffed up his chest. "Like me."

She grumbled under her breath. It was probably true. He had exceptional reflexes, much to her chagrin. He moved like a damn cat.

"And I would never let the ingredients for spaghetti get ruined." He smacked his lips. "It's too precious to waste."

She ignored him and plowed on while trying to open the lid of the tomatoes. "And you almost gave me a heart attack!"

"You're much too young for a heart attack."

"You don't know that," she grunted as she attempted to get the blasted lid off. "For all we know, you could've scared ten years off my life."

Joseph brushed his shaggy blond hair from his face and held his hands out in surrender. "I didn't mean to scare you."

She snorted and gritted her teeth, twisting harder. "Of course you did, or you wouldn't have snuck in here."

He grinned, one side of his mouth turning up. "Okay, you're right. But in my defense, you looked like you needed someone to cheer you up. You looked like a giant raincloud."

Hazel stilled and glanced up at her brother. "I have a lot on my mind."

"Feel like sharing?"

"Not really," she mumbled as she yanked on the jar.

"You need help?"

"No." It was a jar for heaven's sake. She should be able to open it.

Joseph crossed his arms and leaned back against

the sturdy wooden table, crossing his feet at his ankles. That only meant one thing. He was settling in to have a long conversation with her about, God forbid, something serious.

"It doesn't happen to have anything to do with the blending, does it?"

She flicked an annoyed glance in his direction. "Do we really have to do this now?"

"There's not much time left, sis. Make a decision."

Tension tightened her shoulders. Hazel gave up on opening the damn tomatoes and placed the jar into her brother's waiting hands. "And what of Rose? Have you secured her acceptance yet?"

Joseph frowned at her. "It's not that simple. She has children to think of."

"Exactly. Nothing is simple. Nothing."

With a quick flick of his wrist, he opened the tomatoes and held them out to her. She glared at the offending can and snatched it out of his huge hands. "I did all the hard work," she mumbled.

Both siblings stared at each for a beat before bursting out in laughter. Joseph pushed off the table and wrapped his arms around her. Hazel managed to hug him back without dumping the tomatoes all over him. Barely.

"I love you so much, Hazel, and I'm sorry that he's

not here for tomorrow."

She pressed her face into Joseph's shirt, the acute heartache threatening to drown her. "It wasn't supposed to be like this, Jo," she whispered.

"I know, sissy," he soothed, squeezing her tighter.

"What am I supposed to do tomorrow?"

"Trust your head."

She smiled against his shirt. "Not my heart?"

"Never. All that organ ever does is get you into trouble and leave you alone while the object of its desire bears children for a man who doesn't deserve her."

Hazel squeezed her brother back. She wasn't the only one to suffer from loss and heartache. "She was stupid. Hopefully, Rose won't be."

"Naw, Rose is smart. She'll accept my offer."

She pulled back and sat the tomatoes on the counter, then raised a brow at her brother. "That's awfully cocky, brother."

"Not cocky, confident. Her girls are her priority. If we were to marry, her girls would have protection they haven't had since their father died. I can give them that protection."

A bitter laugh escaped her. "What a pair we are. Men are offering for my awkward self to gain power over Harbor, and women are willing to accept your crazy ass because of the protection you can offer."

"I wouldn't call you awkward. Stunted, maybe…" He dodged out of the way when she tried to punch his arm. "And vicious."

"You don't know vicious," Hazel joked, turning back to the counter. "Go bother Brent. I have dinner to prepare."

Jo dropped a kiss on the top of her hair. "No doubt he's started a fire the size of our house."

She sniggered. "He's always been a pyro. Make sure to curb his enthusiasm. I need to be able to get near it to cook."

"'Kay."

Hazel pulled a pot from the shelf underneath the counter and poured the tomatoes into it, lethargy hitting her hard. Today had been exhausting, and the worst was yet to come. She still had to talk to her father about the blending and broach the only subject he wouldn't speak of.

Her mother.

CHAPTER FOUR

Hazel

"Dinner's good, Hazel," Jake said between bites.

She glanced up from her own bowl of spaghetti and smiled at her oldest brother, illuminated by lamplight. "Thank you. When's Katie getting home?"

"Mrs. McShane is in labor, so she won't be home 'til tomorrow."

Hazel hid a smile at his forlorn tone. Her brother was so in love with his loud, crass wife. Instead of choosing a home for themselves, they chose to stay with the family. Katie believed in keeping families together. The wild woman with gray eyes filled the house with laughter and smiles. Hazel counted herself lucky that she'd gained such an amazing sister-in-law.

Her gaze slid to her papa rocking in his chair on the porch, slowly turning a smooth stone in his hand. He was quiet tonight, which ratcheted up her nerves. When her father was quiet, it meant a storm was brewing. She glanced at Joseph, who was whittling away at something. She squinted and grinned at what he was working on. A little cat was forming in his hand.

"Creating storybook characters?" she asked.

Jo glanced in her direction and back to his project. "Cats aren't fairy tales."

"They might as well be," Jake said. "The only cats I've ever seen want to rip my face off and eat me."

"Jake." Her papa's sharp voice cracked through the night air like a whip.

Her brother fell silent and stared into his spaghetti bowl like it held the answers to the world.

She hated it when her father did this. Every time her brothers spoke of the world outside Harbor, he shut them down. He didn't want her to deal with the horrors outside of their walls, but she'd have to deal with them at some time or another. Her hands clenched against the arms of her chair as she watched stars appear in the dark sky. "I wanted to hear what he had to say, Papa," she said softly.

"You don't need to hear about those horrors. It's enough just knowing they're out there."

Her teeth clenched together, but she kept her tone mild. "I need to if I'm to lead Harbor."

"That day is still far off." He studied her for a moment, and then sighed heavily. "It's written all over your face. If you need to say something, just say it."

If only it was that easy. Her stomach churned. "It's about the blending…"

Her papa's rocking ceased; all her brothers seemed to be holding their breath. It had been a sensitive subject in their home since Matt had died. Slowly, he began his rocking while staring up at the dark night sky.

"What about it?" he drawled.

"It's tomorrow."

"True. Your decision is made?"

Her shoulders slumped. The fate of her community rested in her hands, and yet, all she wanted to do was hide from it. "I haven't chosen," she whispered.

"Aaron informed me of that today, baby girl." His tone held unspoken words.

"And?" she said warily. Aaron was her papa's favorite.

"He's concerned that you haven't accepted an offer."

Brent scoffed. "No, he's concerned that you haven't picked him. He was tattling."

"Aaron's a good man," her papa replied. "He's serious, dedicated, smart, and comes from a good family. Hazel would be lucky to marry him."

"He's not a man," she mumbled, staring at the faded slats of wood covering the porch. That was the problem. They were boys. They fought and worked like men, but at the end of the day, their immaturity shone through. How could she entrust them with the safety of all their people?

"What was that?"

She winced at her papa's tone. He hated when she mumbled.

Hazel inhaled and straightened, meeting his narrowed gaze head on. "They're not men, Papa. They're boys parading around like men." She lifted a finger. "One, they don't have any work ethic. Sure, they perform their duties, but do any of them go above and beyond what's necessary?"

He nodded. "They do what they can, but that's something that comes with age, with time."

Time, they didn't have.

"Be that as it may, you've instilled this in all your children. You can't tell me it's an age thing. I was more responsible at the age of eight."

"Showoff," Brent muttered.

Her papa turned his glare on Brent. "Knock it off. This is serious."

When his attention turned back to her, Hazel held up a second finger. "Two, none of them understand our people. They segregate themselves into groups. How can they rule justly when they hold a skewed view of certain people?"

"They must learn, change, and adapt. That's what it means to be part of Harbor."

"Do you think that's really possible?" She didn't. She'd grown up with them. People tended to keep the views ingrained into them as children.

"With the love of a good woman, anything is possible. Your mama made me a better man."

Her throat tightened. There it was. The subtle jab that it was her responsibility to change them, to be the better person and teach them, to be like her mama, but she was nothing like her mama. Her mama had been bubbly and charismatic. People sought her out and wanted to be her friend. People ignored Hazel.

"That brings me to my last point. You and Mama

loved each other. You made each other better."

"What of it?" he asked roughly.

"That's not my future. I'll be attaching myself to a complete stranger." Hazel paused and pushed on: "I take that back. A stranger might not loathe me on sight, but I've grown up with these boys. How can I accept one with how they've treated me? They won't treat me any different once we're married."

Her papa stilled. "They'll treat you with the respect you deserve, or they'll suffer the consequences."

"Damn straight," Jake chimed in.

Hazel appreciated their sentiment, but it wouldn't help anything. "And you expect them to be faithful?"

"You need to believe they will be. If they don't, they will deal with me," her papa said with quiet menace.

She chuckled. "Positive thinking? When has that ever helped? All three of them don't care for me. My peers have teased and tormented me. These boys joined in or stood by idly, doing nothing. Now, I'm just supposed to hope they'll change who they are?"

Her words hung in the air as her papa scrutinized her.

"Hazel, you're a good girl. You always have been, and this is a difficult choice. But it's a choice you need to make. There's no alternative."

"If I waited another year…" She trailed off at the black look on her papa's face.

"We are not having this discussion. Don't bring it up again." He threw his hands in the air and pushed from his chair. "You have a duty to our people."

"I understand, Papa," she said softly. "I'm not trying to get out of anything. It's my duty to marry, but I can't help but think waiting another year would be better."

"You've already pushed it back a year." His tan face softened a touch. "I granted you that since Matt had just died."

"Don't bring Matt into this. This isn't about him. This is about our people and what's best for them."

"And you understand what's best for our people? You who hides in the fields and isolates herself from the people you'll be working with in the future? How would you know?" He leaned a hip against the porch railing, causing it to groan. "This isn't about Harbor. This is about you."

Hazel gazed back at him evenly. He was partly right. She worked in the fields so she could avoid certain people, but that didn't mean she didn't know the people. She was always lending a helping hand when there was a need. Rarely was she thanked, or remembered, but she remembered each person, remembered their stories, and their families.

"It's my blending. It should be about me. This is my life we're talking about. This choice decides who I will spend the rest of my life with."

He shook his head, frowning. "How are you so different?"

"What?"

"You're nothing like your mama. I don't understand it."

All the air seemed to be knocked from her lungs. Heat burned at the back of her eyes and her throat tightened. She dropped her head. That was a low blow. Hazel was acutely aware of how different she was from her mama. Her mama had been outspoken and loved in a way Hazel longed for. A bitter laugh slipped out. The things she learned were because of other people. Her papa barely spoke about her.

A dark, ugly thing rose inside her. She'd always been compared to her mama growing up. No one outright said anything to her, but their whispers followed her all the same.

"How would I know?" she found herself whispering.

"What was that? Speak up, Hazel. I hate mumbling."

She lifted her chin and met his gaze. "I said, 'How

would I know?'"

He stayed silent. Silent like he always did when her mama was brought up. That was the last straw. Her composure broke, and a rush of words flew from her mouth. "How could I ever know what she was like when you never speak of her? Mama died!"

Her papa flinched, but she continued: "But you're the one who took her from me. Once she died, it was like you tried to erase her presence from our lives. The boys have memories of her, but I have almost none. Sometimes, I can't even remember what her face looked like."

She rose from her chair, her arms trembling. "So, if I'm nothing like her, it's on you. Don't blame me for something that wasn't in my power." Her fingers curled into fists. "I love you, but don't you dare judge me. Who I am is a product of your guidance and my decisions. If you don't like it, then blame yourself."

Hazel avoided her brothers' gazes as she moved around them and descended the stairs. She paused at the bottom and turned to stare at her brothers. She loved them, but why did they keep silent? Why did no one say anything? Again, that ugly feeling welled up.

"It's a good thing Mama isn't here. If she was, I wouldn't be the only one she would be disappointed in."

Turning on her heel, she strode away into the darkness. Part of her hoped the darkness would swallow her whole, so she could disappear forever. She skirted around the quiet homes and made her way toward the southern entrance.

You're nothing like her. A tear dripped down her face. Her papa had never said it so plainly before, and it cut deep.

Hazel angrily brushed it off, spying the little tool shed where she kept her weapons. She glanced around through watering eyes and pushed against the heavy, rusted door. It swung inward on silent hinges.

She closed the door, dousing the room in complete darkness. The shed didn't have any windows, but that didn't deter her. Carefully, she edged around a table full of tools and squished between two tall metal shelves. Her fingertips brushed the wall and gently probed until her finger slipped into a little hole. She crooked her finger and pulled. The section of wall pulled out just enough to reveal the cubby where she stashed some of her weapons.

A small smile curled her lips as her hand settled on her sleek Glock 40 and thigh holster. She swallowed hard as she slipped it through her belt loops, and then clasped it around her leg. The weapon had been a gift from her family when she'd come of age. It had been her mother's. Every time she put it on, it was like receiving a hug from her mama.

You're nothing like her.

Bitterness soured her belly as her papa's words echoed through her mind. Maybe she could have been if he hadn't tried to erase every piece of Mama from her life.

She closed the cubby and snatched her bow and quiver from the metal shelf, slinging them over her shoulder. It never hurt to have extra weapons—not that she'd know; she'd never been outside the walls. Her papa and brothers had taught her how to use various weapons, but that was as far as it went. The closest she'd been to danger was when a mutated rattlesnake had surprised her. She'd blown its head off. She'd been proud of herself at the time. Little did she know she'd basically rung a dinner bell. Mutated predators from every direction had raced toward Harbor, all because of a darn snake. That was part of the reason their men hunted with bows and traps. They were quiet. Guns were a last resort.

She slipped out of the shed and closed the door. Maybe she'd find a sneaky hare in the garden. Hare stew was always a favorite in their home. A brisk walk and a good hunt was what she needed to calm down. A fist seemed to close around her throat at the thought of what tomorrow would bring. She exhaled and pushed her shoulders back. Tomorrow would be here soon enough. No need to borrow trouble.

She swung around the corner and jerked to a stop, stifling a shriek. Jo was lounging against the wall of the shed, one foot crossed over the other, looking like the epitome of casualness.

"What are you doing?" she whispered harshly, her heart racing in her chest.

He met her eyes and shoved his hands into his pockets. "Checking on you." A shrug.

Part of her warmed that he cared, but another part iced even further. Suspicion had her narrowing her eyes as she stepped closer to him. "Did Papa send you?"

He scowled at her and shook his head. "No, he didn't. We were worried about you."

Heat built behind her eyes. "You've a funny way of showing it."

"What's that supposed to mean?" he demanded softly.

Hurt and anger pushed to the forefront. "You said

nothing," she choked out. "None of you did."

"What would you have us say? We all have a role to play to survive, Hazel. Nothing we could've said would've changed the decision you're required to make."

"That's not what I'm talking about, Jo."

"I've never heard you speak to Papa that way." He straightened and pushed off the wall. "You were cruel." His tone held disappointment. "You've never been a cruel girl. You're better than that."

She gaped at him, a tear slipping down her cheek. "*I* was cruel?" she gasped. "How dare you! You heard what he said."

"He shouldn't have said those things to you."

"No, he shouldn't have." Her papa's words seemed to be playing in a loop in her mind. *You're nothing like her.* New hurt washed through her. She already knew she was different, that she'd never be able to fill her mama's shoes. She didn't need her papa pointing it out.

"Fighting won't make the pain go away, and tonight's the last night we have together as a family before we have to welcome in your new husband. Don't let an argument ruin your last night. Papa knows he was out of line. Go make peace and let him fix this." He placed both of his hands on top of her shoulders. "And apologize. You both said hurtful things."

The hurt part of her balked at apologizing when her papa was the one in the wrong, but Jo's advice was wise. She'd need her papa's council in the coming months. Leading their community was no easy task. She swallowed hard and tipped her head back to meet her brother's gaze. "I will, but I need to go on a walk to clear my head."

He nodded and pulled her into a rough hug. "I understand. You always seem to do better when you get out of these walls." He squeezed her. "I love you so much, Hazel. We all do. Tomorrow will be a hard day, but don't forget, you've made us proud."

Her lip quivered at his heartfelt sentiment. God, she loved her brothers.

Jo released her and stepped back. His gaze dropped to the gun at her thigh. "I hate that you go past the wall after dark."

She sighed and adjusted her quiver. "Joss won't let me out if there's been danger. I'm always careful. You know I'm not reckless."

"And for that, I'm thankful." He dropped a kiss on top of her head. He pulled a knife from his waist and laid a sheathed blade onto her palm. "Just in case."

She almost rolled her eyes. She already had two of her own knives, but she knew he meant well. Carefully, she attached the blade to her belt loop and lifted a brow. "Happy now?"

"Immensely. The fanatics from that cult called Bayhound have been leveling some threats against Harbor, so keep an eye out."

She gasped. "What? When did this happen? We're at peace with them."

"A couple of days ago. Apparently, a group of Tainted crossed paths with them right before last time we traded. They only arrived with half of what they promised, so we traded for that and went home."

Her brows furrowed. "Then what's the problem?"

"They expected a full payment from us."

Understanding dawned. "They expected you to pay the full price for only half the goods?"

He chuckled bitterly. "Since they sent all the goods, they believe they should receive the full payment."

"But that doesn't make any sense. It's not our fault they weren't able to protect their convoy, and it's not like we cheated them."

"That's not how they see it."

"Idiots," she muttered. People were so dumb

sometimes. "Has Papa begun negotiations?"

"I believe he was thinking it over when you dropped your bomb tonight."

She winced, then planted her hands on her hips. "If someone had told me what's going on, I would have approached the conversation differently."

"Doubtful, but this conversation can wait." He lifted his chin to the wall. "Be safe, and make peace with Papa before you go to bed. He's stewing on the porch already."

A chuckle escaped her. He always stewed on the porch when he said something stupid and guilt plagued him. Well, at least he felt as wretched as she did. "Is he pacing or rocking?"

"Rocking."

A small smile tugged at her lips. Her papa *really* felt bad then. That was something. She'd let him stew a little and then bring a rabbit home as a peace offering. Hazel focused back on her brother when he began to back away.

"Tell Joss hello and that he owes me a game of chess. I'll see you later, sis."

"Will do," she said.

"And, Hazel…?"

She glanced at her brother. "Yeah?"

He smiled at her while walking backwards. "You're kind, compassionate, and honorable, just like Mama. You're more like her than you could ever guess. I think that's what scares Papa the most. You have all of her softness, but none of her hardness and anger at the world, and that's okay. That's how Mama would've wanted it. You're exactly what Harbor needs."

Hazel swallowed hard and blinked back the tears at his unexpected praise. "Love you," she croaked.

"Ditto." He winked at her and then spun on his heel like he hadn't just given her the best gift she'd received in a long time.

Hazel wiped at the corners of her eyes just in case any stray tears decided to sneak out, and smiled at her brother's retreating back. Having a family hurt, but it also healed. Lost in her thoughts, she meandered toward the wall. Jo's kind words helped soothe the hurt, but didn't remove the sting of her papa's words. Jo might have thought Harbor needed kindness, but the truth was apparent. They needed someone strong. Someone with grit. She'd have to dig deep and give them what they needed.

CHAPTER FIVE

Hazel

The blending, a drought, and possible war.

Things seemed to all pile up at once. When it rains, it pours, her grandma used to say. The Bayhound settlement wasn't anything they wanted to mess around with. Their ideologies were built on cleanliness and purity. Cleanliness to the point that if someone dropped a piece of food on the floor, that person was severely beaten, and as for purity ... well, only certain bloodlines were approved to mix. They were useful to have as allies, but as enemies? She shuddered.

She rounded a corner and shook off her unease

when a small light lifted, casting a soft glow on the rickety-looking stairs. Picking up her pace, she pushed aside her thoughts for later and jogged up the stairs toward Joss. The warm breeze ruffled her hair when she reached the top, pulling a smile from her. There was something freeing about standing thirty feet in the air. The fist around her lungs eased a little. Her papa, the blending, and panic didn't seem too bad up here when she could see the dips and crests of the valley.

"Going for a walk?"

She turned to the older man, still smiling. "As long as it's been clear."

"Not a blooming thing," he grumped and stood.

He pulled a sturdy rope from beneath the crate he sat on, tied it onto an anchor, and tossed the end of the rope over the wall.

"That's too bad," she said, hiding a smile. The older man loved a good fight. She adjusted her quiver and slung her bow over her head and back. "Jo says you owe him a game of chess."

"I've been hankering to whoop him again." He grinned at her, bearing a gap-toothed smile.

Hazel grinned as she knelt down and turned onto her belly. "Hopefully, I'll snag an untainted hare or two. Does Sarah need anything from the garden?"

Joss plopped down onto his crate, his forehead wrinkling. "She has plenty of herbs," he commented dryly. "They're hanging all over the place at the moment."

She suppressed a smile at his tone. Sarah was one of the doctors in Harbor. She always had an assortment of herbs drying or stewing in their home.

"But if you happen to catch an extra hare, we wouldn't turn away the meat."

"Gotcha," she said as she scooted backward until her legs dangled over the edge of the wall. She grabbed the roped and smiled at Joss. "I'll see what I can do. See you in a bit."

"Be careful, missy," he warned. "Your papa would have my neck if anything happened to you."

"I'll be careful," she huffed as she began to rappel. "I'm always careful."

"As you should be," his voice carried down to her.

She loved this part. Her stomach caught and erupted in a million butterflies. It was thrilling, but it always went too quickly. Soon enough, her boots touched the red, crusty earth. She straightened, sand crunching beneath her boots, and waved one last time at Joss. She sucked in a deep breath, wet dirt, vegetation, and spices teasing her nose. She loved walking through the farm. It was quiet and peaceful. Slowly she meandered southeast toward the pea trellises and cornfields.

Hazel ran her hand along the pea vines, plucking pods and tossing them into her mouth as she picked her way through the fields. Sweetness burst across her tongue. Peas were one of her favorite vegetables. There was something about eating them right out of the garden that made them taste even better, crunchier. She glanced over her shoulder at the shrinking wall. Each step she took away from Harbor seemed to help her breathe better.

She spied a faded red piece of fabric tied on to one of the trellises. Bingo. She squatted and lifted a vine to check her trap. Her breath hissed out as she got a good look at the rabbit inside. Her nose wrinkled.

Tainted.

The mutated rabbit monster had broken her trap and managed to strangle itself with the remnants. She pulled an arrow from her quiver and crept closer, then held it near the rabbit's eye. The tricky bastards knew how to hold deadly still before attacking their prey, but they still flinched when something neared their eyes. It didn't blink. It was truly dead.

Hazel dropped the arrow back into her quiver and pulled her brother's knife from her pocket. She made quick work of the trap. Reluctantly, she pulled the tainted animal out from underneath the peas. It looked even more grotesque in the moonlight. Instead of two blunt front teeth, it had four razor-sharp ones. She lifted it higher and squinted at its grey fur. It wasn't fur per se, but downy-covered scales. It astounded her that a virus mutated a creature into something *other* so much that it went against its true nature. Bunnies weren't meant to be carnivorous.

Hazel pushed from the dirt, eyed the fence in the distance, and then the wall far behind her. She couldn't bury it here. Who knew what it could do to the soil. And she couldn't take it over the wall. That left her with only one choice—throw it over the fence. Chances are it would attract other predators, but that was the chance she had to take. The rabbit wasn't suitable for eating or burying.

She held it far from her body and strode purposefully toward the fence, weaving through the trellises and into the cornfield. It amazed her how tall the plants grew. Apparently, before WWIII, corn was used in everything, and so genetically-modified that humans couldn't digest it. Her great-great-grandpa hated corn and thought it should only be used as feed for animals on his ranch, but he saw the potential to make money. So, he collaborated with the farmers around his area and they created a type of corn that grew all year long, was healthy for people to eat, and could be used as fuel.

Their super corn spread like wildfire and made them billions in a matter of weeks. But with success comes downfalls. Oil tycoons lost money hand over fist, so they put her great-great-great-grandfather out of business by murdering his partner. The money stopped as quickly as it had come, but it was enough for what he wanted to do. Her wily grandfather saw what the world was coming to, so he again collaborated with the six to build military-grade bunkers beneath their modest ranches and farms. When the world blew up in a big way, it was her great-great-grandfather laughing. He, his family, and his close friends were all safe, along with his corn that would provide fuel to run their generators and help feed whoever was left after the mayhem of WWIII.

Hazel pushed through the last bit of corn, the leaves scratching at her arms, and glanced in both directions. No guards. She frowned. While it was good for her not to be seen, it still seemed odd that there wasn't anyone around. But … no time like the present. She lobbed the tainted rabbit over the double chain-linked fence, and then dusted her hands off on her pants. She'd have to scrub her hands with disinfectant when she got home. The tainted virus was only passed through a bite and blood these days, but who knew what kind of disease that thing was carrying.

She froze when movement caught her eye farther down the fence. Guards. Her father might have allowed her walks, but that didn't mean he sanctioned them. Hazel slipped back into the corn and moved away from the fence at a diagonal. She stilled when voices neared her.

"Did you hear that?" a deep male voice asked.

She held her breath and didn't move a muscle as the corn swayed around in the night breeze. Guards tended to shoot first and ask questions later. Not that she remembered anyone getting shot while out in the garden, but no one ever snuck out after dark, either. She'd never seen a single soul out here except for the guards. Terror iced her veins. What if they assumed she was one of the Tainted?

"I didn't hear anything," another male voice said, sounding annoyed.

"I swear, I did." The deep voice sounded even

closer.

"You're wasting time. We have to go."

Her brows furrowed. Go?

"Come on out or we'll shoot," the deep voice called.

"How's that going to help?" a familiar female voice snapped.

"If it's Tainted, it wouldn't understand us. If someone from Harbor, they'd be stupid not to obey."

Hazel sighed. Her papa would kill her for being caught. Every once in a while, the guards would spot her, but generally they ignored her.

"It's just me," she called, and slowly edged her way back toward the fence. She blinked when she stumbled into a small pocket of open space in the cornfield. Her mouth bobbed and then closed as she scanned the unwelcome familiar faces.

"Well, well, well, what do we have here?" Jessy drawled.

Of all the people to catch her ... of all the dumb luck. She tilted her head back and stared at the night sky, wishing for the people in front of her to disappear. She dropped her chin and stifled a groan. Nope, still there. Jessy, Colton, Aaron, and Genevieve all stared at her. Double damn.

Hazel lifted a hand and waved. "Hey, guys," she

said awkwardly. This night couldn't get any worse. What were the chances that all three of the guys who had proposed to her would be together and stumble across her? Bad luck, that's what it was.

Aaron crossed his arms across his chest and arched an eyebrow. "Are you going to tell us why you're out here?"

"Does it matter?" Gen sniped, tossing a glare her way. "Who knows why she does what she does?"

Typical Gen, so generic a jibe that Hazel thought her brain would seep from her eyes. Could she be more unoriginal? For sure, Gen's favorite color was white, and vanilla her favorite flavor of ice cream.

Colton stepped closer with a twinkle in his eye and gestured to her bow. "Obviously, she's out hunting."

"You sure she can use it?" Jessy teased. Gen sniggered.

Something inside her snapped. Her eyes turned to slits as she gazed at Jessy. Jo was right. Jessy was a dirtbag. He'd been a constant thorn in her side for the last couple of years. There was no way in hell she'd marry him. She wouldn't put up with this. She was his future leader, and he'd better show some respect.

"I can show you better than I can tell you," she purred, not sounding anything like herself.

In one smooth motion she pulled the bow from her shoulder, an arrow from her quiver, nocked it and loosed. A smug smile tugged at her lips as Jessy gaped at the arrow embedded in the dirt between his legs.

He yipped and covered himself while hopping back a few paces. "You could have hit me!"

"You're right, but I didn't," she replied, her tone cool.

"Kitten has claws." Colton smirked and wiggled his eyebrows. "Who knew you were so feisty?"

Hazel rolled her eyes and slung her bow over her shoulder. Once a playboy, always a playboy. "I should be getting back. I'll see y'all tomorrow." She was curious as to why they were out there, but not curious enough to stick around.

"Hazel…" Aaron's deep voice washed over her.

"Yeah?" She met his deep brown gaze.

"We're celebrating the blending tonight. Come with us."

"A celebration?" she said slowly. Where were they having a celebration?

"It'll be fun," Colton added with a wink. "Come on, let loose. We're only young once, and tomorrow everything will change."

"Um … I don't know…" Why were they inviting her

anyway? She almost snorted.

Because all three guys wanted to marry her.

"Why invite her?" Gen whined. "It's not like she knows how to have fun anyway. She'll ruin the night."

"I'll go," she blurted. Immediately, she wanted to kick herself. She wouldn't have fun with any of them. How did she backpedal out of this situation? "Are Baz and Mesa invited?" she asked. If they weren't going, then she could use them as an out.

"I'm sure they're already there," Jessy said. "I would be if I was blending with Mesa tomorrow."

Hazel glared at Jessy and hid her surprise when Aaron reached out and slapped Jessy on the back of his dirty-blond head. "Have some respect."

That warmed Hazel up to Aaron a bit. She shifted from side to side. "So, where are we going?"

"You'll see," Gen said darkly, and turned on her heel to stalk out of the little clearing. Jessy tossed a dirty look over his shoulder and followed her.

Colton shook his head. "She's always so moody." He waved a hand at Hazel. "Follow us."

With reluctant steps, she trailed after Colton through the corn, followed by Aaron. A million questions hovered on the tip of her tongue. Where was the celebration? Why were they sneaking around in the corn? The skin between her shoulder blades prickled as they traveled further into the corn and she hid a shiver. She hated being stared at.

"I didn't peg you for a rule breaker," Aaron muttered from behind her.

Hazel kept her eyes forward to avoid being smacked with an ear of corn. "I needed to go for a walk."

"Outside the wall?"

"It's freeing out here."

A pause. "I feel the same. There's something about being outside of Harbor that calms me."

She lifted her eyebrows, staring at Colton's back. "It calms me, too."

"Bound to happen."

"What?" she asked, batting a leaf out of her face.

"That we'd have something in common."

She stiffened, but he didn't continue the conversation, much to her relief. She didn't want to think about husbands right at this moment. She halted when Colton paused in front of her and then stooped down to crawl through something. Hazel took a step back when she got a clear view of what it was.

The moonlight gleaming on the fence ... there was a hole cut through it. A hole. She swallowed hard as

Gen, Colton, and Jessy stared at her from outside the perimeter.

There was a bloody hole in the fence.

"What in the world?" she whispered. "What is this?"

"You didn't think the celebration would be inside Harbor, did you?" Jessy asked with arched brows.

"I don't know what I thought," Hazel said, still staring at the hole cut in the fence. "Did you guys do this?" If her papa found out, he'd be furious.

Colton laughed quietly while eyeing the surrounding area. "We're not the first to sneak out before the blending. This has been a tradition for years."

"How have I not heard of this?" she asked no one in particular. "How has my father not put a stop to this?"

"Hazel…"

She blinked and peeked over her shoulder at Aaron, feeling off balance. They wanted her to leave Harbor. "Yeah?"

"This is your decision. You don't have to go, but we are." He turned her around to face him and stared down at her, his warm palms on her shoulders. "I think it would be a good idea for you to go. Everyone will be there, *your* future people. This might pave the way to an easier transition for you."

He said for *you*, but she heard for *us*. She stared at his green t-shirt pulled tightly across his chest. Was she really going to do this? The freedom she'd craved for so long was within her grasp, and Aaron was right. It would be a good opportunity to be seen as normal, as one of them. She glanced over her shoulder at the fence. She'd always wanted to go out. A part of her cried out to see what lay outside the fence.

What about her family? Guilt churned in her gut. Would they be worried about her? "How long will we be gone?"

"Not long enough to cause any panic."

She chewed on her lip. Her papa would strangle her if he knew what she was pondering, but she knew her answer the moment they invited her. Maybe her papa would understand?

That, or he'd lock her up for a hundred years.

Hazel blew out a breath and tipped her head back to smile at Aaron. The blending was tomorrow. Her papa wouldn't be looking for her anywhere. Maybe she hadn't been looking at the blending right. Maybe it wasn't a cage, but freedom.

Pulling in a deep breath, she turned back to the fence. "Let's go."

CHAPTER SIX

Hazel

As soon as the words passed her lips, her body flashed hot and cold, and her fingers began to numb. That was a bad sign, wasn't it?

She curled her fingers into fists and stared at the cut in the fence. Finally, she would leave. What was out there? What would it be like? Was she making the biggest mistake of her life?

"Hazel?" A tug on her bow pulled her from her thoughts.

She puffed out a breath and allowed Aaron to pull the bow and quiver from her shoulder. He slung it over his own shoulder and placed a hand at the curve of her back.

"We have to go," he whispered softly. "You can change your mind. You don't have to go. No one will judge you."

That was a blatant lie.

Her gaze slid to the others outside the fence. Gen would harass her for years to come if she didn't, but that didn't sway her. No amount of peer pressure would force her to do something she didn't want to do. She *needed* to go. "No, I want to come." She rolled her neck. "Here goes nothing," she muttered.

Bending low, she pushed through the first chain-link fence and then the second, the metal scraping the exposed skin of her arms. Hazel stumbled to her feet and spun around to stare wide-eyed at Aaron on the other side. She did it. She'd left Harbor. Part of her wanted to dance around and whoop for joy; the other part of her wanted to crawl back through the fence, go home, and get into her bed. But that option disappeared as Aaron laid her bow and quiver on the ground and began to wiggle through.

"Wait." She stepped forward and held her hands out. "Hand me my bow, please."

"You don't need it," Aaron said from the ground. "We have plenty of weapons."

That made her frown. "We're in the wilds. There's no such things as too many weapons." She gestured to the gun at her thigh. "Plus, this is veritably useless."

He stared at her for a beat and then sighed, shuffling backwards. He handed over her bow and quiver and then wiggled through. Hazel watched in interest as he pulled zip ties from his back pockets and snapped them into place, closing the fence. There was no going back now.

She glanced around them and spun in a circle as she took everything in. Everything looked the same but felt completely different. A smile curled her lips. She was outside the fence. Fear and excitement caused goosebumps to break out on her arms. Unconsciously, her hand brushed the Glock at her thigh and her right hand tightened around her bow.

"How safe are we?"

She ignored the mocking smiles of Gen and Jessy, and pinned Aaron with a glance, who watched her quietly.

He shrugged a shoulder. "The area's been swept already. We also have guards stationed along the route. The celebration is not far from here. Despite the horror stories, our valley is quite safe."

Matt's face flashed through her mind. *Not safe*

enough. But she kept those words firmly inside. She slung her quiver over her head and shouldered her bow while battling with the grief that threatened to overwhelm her.

"Can we go yet?" Jessy griped.

Colton rolled his eyes and strode toward the forest. "Hold your horses. We'll get there when we get there. Give the girl a chance to get her bearings."

"She wouldn't be getting her bearings if she'd done her duty like the rest of us," Jessy grumbled.

A flush worked up her chest. Her father had done her no favors keeping her inside. She worked hard for Harbor, but she had also received special treatment even though she never asked for it, nor wanted it.

"Shut up," Colton said. "She did her duty like everyone else."

"If you say so," Gen sniped.

"Enough," Aaron commanded, strolling up to her side.

She peeked up at him, feeling out of sorts and self-conscious.

His hardened gaze met hers and softened a touch. "You ready?"

"As ready as I'll ever be," she murmured.

He squinted at her like he was trying to read her

mind. He must have found what he was looking for, because he nodded and again gave her a little nudge forward. "This area has been cleared, but you still need to keep an eye out. Safety is just an illusion out here."

She swallowed and picked up her pace, her gaze darting left to right. There was no way she wanted to be left behind once they entered the forest.

Hazel hesitated only a moment at the tree line. Her gaze flickered back to the open field before she turned and stepped into the forest. A deeper darkness settled over her as the large trees blotted out the moonlight. Her eyes adjusted, and she stifled her gasp. It was beautiful. Trees stood like giants above her, twisting together to form what looked like some sort of pagan dance.

"Do you like it?" Aaron asked quietly from behind her.

"It's lovely," she breathed, while moving forward. Her breath caught when she rounded a lichen-covered tree, and for the first time, she saw her creek. A small break in the foliage allowed moonlight to shine through, causing the creek's surface to glimmer like it held a million crystals. Her pace picked up until she stood at the water's edge. Fine sand faded into smooth multi-colored stones that decorated the bottom of the creek.

This was worth the risk. It was more beautiful than she'd ever imagined. Even if this was the only thing she got to experience tonight, it was worth it.

She squatted and reached a hand out toward the water. Aaron's tanned hand wrapped around her wrist and pulled it back. She glanced up at him in surprise.

"It's dangerous, Hazel. Venomous fish and snakes like to hide underneath those smooth rocks. You wouldn't even see one before it bit you."

Wide-eyed, she glanced back at the creek. "But it's so beautiful."

"Most dangerous things are." He gently tugged at her hand, pulling her to her feet. "There's a log bridge over here. We'll cross there."

He dropped her hand and she followed him, casting incredulous looks at their surroundings. She'd dreamed of this moment for so long, but never thought she'd see it realized.

Aaron paused when he came to a huge tree that had fallen over the creek. He glanced over his shoulder at her. "Do you have good balance?"

She smiled and moved past him without

answering. Since she was a little girl, she had been climbing onto their porch railing and walking the edges. She'd about given her mama a heart attack the first time she did it. Aaron cursed and followed her. He didn't have anything to worry about; the creek was only seven feet wide, and the tree trunk was huge.

For a wicked moment, she thought about doing a cartwheel across the log, but reason grabbed hold of her. Aaron didn't deserve to be scared like that, and there was always a chance an accident could happen. It only took a few steps to cross before she hopped to the ground and grinned at Aaron as he landed beside her.

"A simple yes would have sufficed," he muttered, looking severely put out.

"Sorry." She wasn't, but he was clearly upset. In a move uncharacteristic of her, she popped onto her toes and placed a kissed on his whiskered cheek.

His eyes widened and then shuttered. "What was that for?" he asked.

"For bringing me out here." She glanced around and then back to him. "It's like a fairy tale."

He shook his head. "You're so ... fanciful."

"Sometimes." She shrugged, trying not to be affected. His words bit. They were all too close to something her father would say, but she wouldn't let them dampen her evening. As it was, she was filing away each second, so she could relive each moment in the future. "If you're always serious, how will you find joy in life?" she asked, striding forward.

"It wasn't a criticism, Hazel," he said, matching her pace.

"It sounded like one," she murmured, soaking in the sights.

"I meant you're different."

She arched a brow at him.

"You better stop before you dig yourself too deep," Colton called from ahead of them. "Holes are hard to get out of."

Aaron rolled his eyes. "Different is good."

She hid her smile and nodded. Silence descended over them as they weaved through more trees and stopped when they reached the rest of the group. Hazel gaped and pointed a finger at the vehicle they were pulling tarps off of.

"Is that a Jeep?" she asked.

"It says Jeep," Gen drawled, pointing to the rusted emblem.

"How?"

"It's my dad's," Colton said, slipping into the

driver's seat. "He managed to finagle this from those fanatics years ago. He keeps it here for personal use."

Hazel eyed the gasoline-run vehicle with no doors. "And it won't blow up on us?" Gasoline was a thing of the past. From her studies, she knew it was highly unstable, unlike the corn-based fuel they used now.

"It's safe," Jessy commented from the front seat.

"And it hasn't gone bad?"

"It's not like it's a vegetable," Colton quipped.

"You know what I mean," Hazel said.

"Get in, founder girl, or go back," Jessy snarked.

She ignored his taunt and circled the Jeep. He would not heckle her into something that might kill her. She glanced up and met Gen's narrowed gaze as Gen slid into the middle seat. That settled it for her. Gen was a self-centered brat. There's no way she would sacrifice herself just to go out to a party. Gen liked herself too much.

Hazel pulled her bow off her shoulder, wrapped her hand around the dirty roll bar, and pulled herself into the small back seat. She winced as the cracked leather poked through her thin tank-top and her quiver pushed into her back. Shifting to the side, she bumped into Gen and offered her an apologetic smile. She jumped when a finger brushed her bare shoulder.

Hazel followed the arm back to Aaron, who lifted his chin at her. Huh? What did that mean?

"You ready?"

That's what it meant.

"Yeah," she said nervously.

Colton grinned at her from the cracked rear-view mirror. "Let's see if she'll run for us."

She gaped and braced herself, placing her bow across her lap. Oh, God. It wasn't the Tainted or her father that was going to get her; it was a gasoline-run machine.

The Jeep didn't so much as clunk; it turned over and purred. Colton jerked it into gear and soon they were bumping along the path. She leaned forward, her fingers wrapping around the headrest, and asked, "Can't the guards hear the engine?"

Colton shook his head. "They can, but they've been paid off."

Her eyebrows rose, and she darted a look at Aaron, but he wasn't looking in her direction. He was listening to something Gen was whispering in his ear.

"You have a problem with paying the guards, sweet thing?" Jessy asked.

"No," said Hazel slowly. "I'm just surprised is all."

He snorted. "I'm not surprised. I'm sure you have a

skewed view of what Harbor's really like. You're naïve."

"I'm not naïve." Hazel glanced away from him as they left the forest and began driving across the red sand littered with spiny plants and outcroppings of sandstone rocks.

"So says the girl who's never been outside our walls."

"So says the girl who works harder than most for Harbor and helps those that the rest of the people deem unworthy of their attention." She glanced around the vehicle when everyone went silent.

Colton glanced at her in the rear-view mirror. "You've lived a privileged life, and you get a choice."

"I'm not debating that I've led a privileged life, but with that life comes more responsibility." She chuckled bitterly. "As for a choice, I'm just as helpless as y'all. We have to survive, and to do so, things must be done a certain way. I don't get to choose any more than you do."

"You get to choose who you marry," Gen said, crossing her arms. "Most of us marry whoever can afford us the best protection."

"You think I'm any different?" Hazel met her angry gaze and shook her head. "I'm not. I have to choose someone who will benefit Harbor as a whole. What I want doesn't even matter."

"And what do you want?" Aaron asked quietly.

"Freedom," she whispered, watching the moonlight-painted earth rush past them. "But I'll settle on someone who will put others first."

"Speaking of which, have you made a decision?" Colton asked carefully.

Tension thickened around them; the fist around her lungs tightened, threatening to suffocate her. "No."

She had.

She knew from the beginning who it would be. Hazel just didn't want to admit it to herself. Leaving Harbor just confirmed it. Jessy was always out of the question. He didn't care for anyone but himself. Colton was quirky and courageous, but his gaze wandered too much. She'd seen him with women. Harbor needed someone who was stable, or at least discreet.

That left Aaron.

She swallowed hard and squinted at the copse of trees in the distance. He was as responsible as he could be at his age. With time, he'd turn into the perfect little copy of her papa. Not that there was anything wrong with her papa. She loved him, but she didn't want to be married to him. At least she knew what being married to Aaron would be like.

There wouldn't be any surprises.

Hazel brushed the hair from her face and placed her cheek against the back of Colton's headrest. She let herself drift in her thoughts of everything and nothing as they traveled along a gully dotted with cactus and sagebrush. To some it might be ugly, but to her it was the most beautiful thing she'd ever seen. The moonlight brushed along red stone arches, turning them a violet color that would be forever seared into her mind.

Even if she couldn't have the freedom she longed for, she had tonight, and Aaron had given that to her. The others wouldn't have invited her. It was a calculated move to get what he wanted, but Hazel appreciated it anyway. It was an unexpected gift, one she'd always treasure.

Colton weaved around rocks like he'd done this a million times before. He probably had. Trees seemed to sprout from nowhere and her open view was cut off. Her body slid forward as Colton slowed to a stop and cut the engine. He hopped out and threw his arms open wide. "Your party awaits, my lady."

She rolled her eyes and hopped out of the Jeep, smiling despite herself, and swung her bow over her shoulder. He was a man-whore, but he had style. She'd give him that much. After the ride, the silence seemed so much louder. She cocked her head and listened. It wasn't completely silent. There was faint music.

Jessy shoved a grinning Colton and headed off toward the music without so much as a backward glance. Colton held his arm out to her. "May I escort you?"

"What the heck." She threw her hands in the air and looped her arm through his. "Why thank you, kind sir. What I would do without your guidance?"

His eyebrows rose, and his smile grew. "Here, I thought you were a stick in the mud."

"And here, I thought you were a rake." She arched an eyebrow of her own. "And I was right."

His teeth flashed at her in the darkness. "You are too perceptive."

She shrugged and followed his lead as he directed them through trees.

"You know," he said slowly, "we would make a great-looking couple."

Hazel steeled herself for the pitch that was surely coming her way. "Oh, yeah?"

"We would make pretty babies."

"I'm sure, as I'm also sure mine would not be the *only* pretty babies."

He glanced down at her sharply. "You don't think I can be faithful?"

She shrugged a shoulder, spying firelight in the distance. "You forget that I've been raised with you. You may not know me, but I'm well aware of you and your reputation."

"Life with me would be fun," he added with a wiggle of his eyebrows.

That did make her grin. "I can imagine, but Harbor needs stability, not fun."

He nodded and stared toward the light. "You're not what I imagined."

"I doubt you've spent your time imagining me."

"You're right to a point, but I like mysteries. You're a founder's daughter and yet you blended right into the walls. I can't remember a time where you stuck out."

"Thanks," she said dryly.

"I didn't mean it negatively. I meant that you're an enigma. Not good, not bad, just different." He looked over his shoulder and back to her face. "So, it's Aaron?"

"Seems that way," she murmured.

Colton pursed his lips like he had something to say.

Hazel grinned. "Come on. You've been brutally honest until this point. Why hold back?"

"He's not fun."

"Yep." He'd always been in the popular crowd, but it looked like he never enjoyed it. He was what she liked to call a perpetual frowner.

"He wants power."

"That's nothing new." Everyone wanted power.

Colton blew out a breath. "He's a cold fish. Be careful."

Hazel eyed Colton. That was unexpected. "I will. Thanks for the warning."

What an odd evening. Colton had never said more than a handful of words to her and here he was warning her about another guy.

"It's the least I could do for my almost-wife."

She giggled and slapped her hand over her mouth. What. The. Heck? She hardly ever giggled. It was all too much. She'd broken out of Harbor, left with people who had never looked her way, and now Colton was flirting with her. It was like being in an alternate universe.

Colton grinned down at her, flashing white teeth in

the darkness. "Why Hazel, I never guessed you'd have such a charming laugh."

An embarrassing snort escaped, followed by more giggles. "I'm so sorry," she managed to get out between laughs. "It's just so surreal. Maybe I'm dreaming."

He wiggled his eyebrows at her again. "You dream about me at night?"

Hazel snorted again and slapped his arm. "You wish."

"You know it," he teased.

She shook her head and focused on the firelight peeking in between the foliage ahead, the music growing louder. That sobered her. Apprehension stirred in her chest. What would everyone think when they saw her? Most likely, they'd stare and make comments under their breath. The comments she could handle. It was the stares that bothered her. She went unnoticed most of the time, and when someone did notice her, it was to ridicule her. Her stomach churned.

"Hey, you okay?" Colton asked softly.

"Yeah, I'm fine," she said.

"Your grasp says differently."

She glanced down to her fingers digging into his

arm and released her hold on him. "Sorry."

He snatched her hand back before she pulled completely away and again weaved her arm through his. "It's no problem. I don't need that arm anyway, especially if I get to walk into the party with a beautiful girl clinging to it."

"Clinging is an understatement," she mumbled.

"They're just people," he said, pulling her closer to the light.

She stiffened as voices began to trickle through the trees.

"Wipe that look from your face right now."

Hazel's gaze snapped to his face.

He paused just outside the meadow. "You look scared, miserable, and stuck-up all at once." His opposite hand touched a corner of her mouth. "Smile, Hazel."

She forced a smile for him.

"It looks like you're being tortured."

"That's because I am," she muttered, earning a smile from Colton that she mirrored.

His smile grew. "There it is. That's the smile you want to show everyone."

"Are you serious?" Gen stomped through the trees, Aaron trailing behind her. She smirked and tossed her hair over her shoulder. "Smiling won't change who she is." With that parting remark, she sauntered through the shrubs and into the meadow.

"Ignore her," Aaron grumbled. "I do."

That startled a laugh out of her at the unexpected joke. At least, she thought it was a joke. She squared her shoulders and lifted her chin. "I can do this."

"Yes, you can. Let's go, princess," Colton said.

Taking the final step into the meadow wasn't as hard as she thought it would be, and much to her relief no one threw her out. What surprised her most was the amount of people dancing in the firelight and drinking. How did they manage to get away with this?

"Breathe, Hazel."

She released the breath she didn't know she was holding and smiled as pleasantly as she could as people noticed her.

"Well, sweet, sweet, almost-wife, do you want me to introduce you to anyone?"

"Heck, no," she said, peeking up at him through her lashes. "I'm going to find myself a quiet corner with Baz and Mesa and enjoy the evening."

"I figured as much." He leaned closer and surprised the heck out of her by brushing a kiss along her cheek.

She jerked and tried not to gape at him. "What was

that for?"

"To keep them guessing. Never let them see you sweat."

He pulled her hand from his arm and squeezed once before strolling into the gaping crowd. Part of her wanted to giggle at the wide-eyed disbelief. She ignored the looks and searched the crowd for Baz and Mesa, but she couldn't see them anywhere. Baz was so tall, he was hard to miss.

"You sure Baz and Mesa are here?" she asked Aaron, who had planted himself by her side.

"Baz and Mesa wouldn't miss this for anything."

She flicked a look in his direction before resuming her search. "What makes you say that?"

"It's a guy thing."

"Un huh," she said, eyeing the mass of dancing people. "I'm going to walk around the meadow and see if I can find them. If not ... I'm going in."

Aaron snorted. "Good luck with that."

She saluted like the dork she was and wandered around the grove. People lounged on blankets playing games, talking, celebrating. Each group she passed sent curious glances her way, but no one was downright rude. That was a first. Maybe it was because she'd arrived with the others. Tonight, by far, had been the warmest welcome she'd received in a long time.

The firelight twisted and snaked through the air, casting dancing shadows against the silent trees that stood as gentle giants above them. It was something she'd add to her collection of memories to turn over in her mind when things were bad in the future. Beauty of that sort could make the grumpiest person downright chipper.

She scowled when she caught sight of Aaron standing in the same spot, now surrounded by a group of people. Darn it. She glanced at the mass of people swaying to the beat. Either she could stand here all night, or she could enter the fray and find her friends. A small smile tugged on her lips. On the plus side, she loved to dance.

She propped her bow and quiver next to a tree, began to sway her hips to the beat, then took the plunge by slowly dancing her way into the crowd. Her breaths came in big puffs of air as bodies crushed her from all sides. Hands brushed her arms, face, and waist as she danced further into the crowd. Then, a familiar face entered her line of vision.

Colton's head was thrown back as a group of girls surrounded him, all pawing at his shirt. She sniggered and kept dancing. They reminded her of a pack of wolves surrounding their prey. It wasn't until he dropped his head and caught her eye that she knew she was wrong. He smoothly disentangled himself from the girls and took three prowling steps to reach her. He was the wolf, not the prey.

He grinned and pulled her against him. She lightly placed her hands on his chest and followed his lead to the music. "Here I thought a good little girl like you couldn't dance," he said with a roguish grin.

"Never said I couldn't," she said, shimmying out of his grasp. He grinned and took a step closer, interest glinting in his gaze. Hazel waved a finger at him and danced away, laughing. "I need to find my friends."

He jerked his chin to her right. "I saw Baz in that direction."

"Thanks," she called over the loud music.

Sweat dewed the back of her neck as she swiveled her hips and danced her way through the crowd. She'd never felt so free. So happy. Right now, she was in the moment. No responsibility. No shame. Just happiness and freedom. Hazel threw her head back and lifted her hands into the air, enjoying it.

"Hazel?"

Her eyes popped open at her name and twisted to

smile at Baz. Mesa was frozen in his arms, her mouth hanging wide open.

"Surprise!" she said, sashaying toward them.

Mesa abandoned her ice sculpture impression and shook her head. "What are you doing here?" she asked, wrapping Hazel in a hug.

"Celebrating." She pulled back and smiled at Mesa's huge aqua eyes.

"How did you get here?"

Hazel's smile waned a touch. "An acquaintance."

Baz crowded in, eyebrows raised. "Your father is going to kill you."

A sick feeling swirled in her gut, taking with it part of her happy glow. She glanced between the stern faces of her friends and reached for each of their hands. "Look, I know it's a surprise to find me here..." She raised both her eyebrows. "I'm not going to question why *you* didn't invite me yourself..." She ignored both of their sheepish expressions. "But I know why you didn't. I wouldn't have come."

"Then why did you?" Mesa asked.

Hazel glanced to the side, the gyrating bodies around them blurring and rolling. "Because I needed one night for myself before I buckle down and live for Harbor." She turned back to her friends and forced a wobbly smile onto her face. "I made my decision. I'm ready for it, really I am, but tonight is for me. Tomorrow will be here soon enough, but for tonight? Tonight, I want to celebrate and dance. Will you dance with me?"

Baz was the first one to crack a smile. He twirled her around and reached for Mesa with his other hand. "I, for one, won't turn a pretty lady down. I say I'm the lucky one. I get to dance with the two most beautiful girls here."

Something loosened inside her chest as Mesa melted and shimmied toward her. Her best friend placed a kiss on her cheek and met her eyes.

"Tonight, we dance, and tomorrow, we stand together."

Hazel jerked her head up and down. Standing for Mesa and Baz would be one of the easiest things she'd ever do.

Baz lifted their hands in the air and shook his hips while wiggling his eyebrows. "Enough seriousness. Let loose, and let the fun begin."

CHAPTER SEVEN

Hazel

Her stomach muscles hurt from laughing so much.

Baz had twirled them around and around. It was an absolute blast, and at no time did she feel like a third wheel. Her self-consciousness melted away the longer they danced. A few times, she'd danced with guys and girls she'd met over the years, and no one protested one bit.

Baz dipped her and spun her out of his arms to pull Mesa close again. Hazel smiled at the love on their faces. At least something wonderful would come out of the blending tomorrow.

She rolled her hips and caressed her sides as she

lifted her hands in the air. Masculine hands settled on her waist and a chest touched her back. She let him lead her for a while before she spun around and almost tripped over her own feet.

Dark, serious brown eyes met hers. She blushed and focused on dancing with the music while looking anywhere but at Aaron's face.

"Are you not going to look at me?"

She forced herself to look into his face. "I just didn't expect it to be you. You don't seem the..."

"Fun-having type?" he tacked on, pulling her a little closer.

Her nose crinkled. "Those are your words, not mine. I was going to say dancing type."

A smile cracked his stony expression. "Dancing is a great way to get close to pretty girls."

"Mmmhmm," she hummed, placing her hands on his biceps. It was clearly a line, but it still warmed her inside nonetheless. When was the last time a male had said she was pretty other than her family?

Matt.

Her throat closed up; heat suddenly pressed from behind her eyes. She scanned the crowd as they blurred around her. He would have loved it here. Aaron leaned closer and brushed his thumb underneath her eye. Oh, hell. Mortification washed over her. She was crying. How pathetic.

"Come on, let's go cool down," he said, taking her hand, leading her out of the crowd.

Cool air rushed over her skin when they parted from the dancing frenzy; she swallowed over and over to clear the lump that had formed in her throat. Matt seemed to haunt her every thought in the last week. Everything reminded her of him.

Aaron paused and let go of her hand. "Are you thirsty?"

She nodded, not trusting herself to speak.

"I'll grab you a water."

As soon as he dropped her hand and strode toward a cooler, she swiped at the tears making an escape despite her wishes. Leave it to her to cry when she was so happy. She inhaled deeply.

Get it together, Bresh.

Aaron weaved around stargazing, paired-off couples and wordlessly handed her the water.

"Thanks," she croaked before taking a small sip. She bit her lip and glanced at the ground, her emotions all over the place. She flinched when Aaron stepped into her space and cupped her chin, forcing her to meet his eyes.

"It's okay."

Hazel nodded jerkily, and then froze when she

caught Gen and her posse glaring in their direction from the corner of her eye. That's the last thing she needed.

Aaron noticed her attention and followed her gaze. He scowled and stepped back, holding his hand out to her. "You wanna sit for a little bit?"

He was offering a lifeline. "Sure," she whispered and took his hand.

He led her into the forest and wove around a few trees until they reached a secluded spot. She shifted on her feet and glanced back toward the party. It was close enough that she could still hear the music and see the firelight, but far enough away that no one could overhear quietly-spoken words. Aaron released her hand and sat on a fallen log and patted the spot beside him.

Here goes nothing.

Hazel followed his lead and plopped down beside him with enough space between them that they didn't touch. Silence descended around them. It should've been uncomfortable, but it wasn't. She was grateful he didn't force her to speak. Slowly, she wrangled control of her emotions and studied Aaron out of the corner of her eye, her cheeks still burning. They'd only exchanged a few sentences until this point, and she'd already cried around him. If only she had disappearing powers.

"So, you going to tell me what those tears were about?" he asked, breaking the silence. He glanced from his hands to the side of her face.

No, she most certainly did not. If she opened up now, she might never stop crying. She shrugged a shoulder. "Not much to say."

"I don't think that's the case, but I'll let it go for now." He clasped his hand between his knees. "How about something easier? You and Colton?"

Nothing about this conversation would be easy. "What gave you that idea?" she asked, not giving anything away. Her papa always said to never give information for free. It was currency, like anything else.

"You looked pretty chummy together. I could only hear snippets of your conversation, but it seemed like y'all hit it off."

Interesting. She angled herself toward him, her knee almost brushing his, and raised a brow. "You eavesdropped?"

Aaron rolled his eyes. "We were walking behind you. It was hard not to hear some things."

"I just bet," she replied, not taking his bait. If he wanted an answer, he would have to ask her outright. There was no way she'd make it easy on him.

He chuckled and turned towards her to straddle their makeshift bench. "Have you made your decision? Are you marrying Colton?"

That was a straight as you could get. Her heart thundered, and her throat grew dry, but it was surprisingly easy to say the words she'd been dreading for months. The moment was finally here.

"Yes, I've made my decision."

She was going to puke.

"Can I make one last appeal?"

He thought she'd chosen Colton. Hazel swallowed against the nerves that threatened to leave her mute. "There's no need. I chose you, Aaron." There. It was done. There was no backing out now, and her voice only wobbled a little.

Aaron blinked slowly. "That's not the answer I was expecting." He barked out a laugh. "I prepared a speech and everything." He ran a hand through his hair and straightened, meeting her gaze. "You made a good decision."

Did she? Only time would tell. Hazel tried to smile at him, but it felt wrong on her face.

"You don't need to do that."

"What?" she asked through numb lips.

"Pretend you're happy."

A blush crept up her neck. Hell, she was being so

rude. "I meant no offense…"

He held up a hand. "You don't need to explain anything to me, Hazel. We're both reasonable adults. There's no need to make platitudes or lie to each other. The only way this will work is if we're honest with each other. I'll start … I'm not an emotional person. I'm stubborn and I like to get my way. Now you…"

Well, that was honest and unexpected. She pursed her lips and tried to think of something good. "I'm a crier," she blurted. "It happens if I'm mad, hurt, angry, or sad. Everything inconveniently shows itself in the form of tears."

"Good to know."

He squinted at her and then pulled a flask from his back pocket and held it out to her.

"Moonshine?" she guessed. Her brothers raved about Aaron's family's moonshine.

"Is there anything else?"

Hazel smiled and shook her head. "I'm good."

"Suit yourself." He took a pull from it, then wiped the back of his mouth with his hand and sat the flask between them. "I needed a little liquid courage before my next confession." A pause. "I've always planned on marrying you."

Her jaw dropped. Say what? She snapped her

mouth closed and crossed her arms. "Now *that* I find hard to believe."

"Why is that?"

Hazel snorted. "You've never looked my way. We've practically been raised together, and not once did you linger."

He shook his head ruefully. "I tried a few times, but Matt was always at your side. You were blind to everyone else."

Just hearing his name made her ache. She rubbed a hand over her chest and stared at the flask between them. People always said time would heal all wounds, but they were full of crap. Nothing would heal the pain, but she knew it would fade. "I miss him."

"You've been different since he died."

"Death changes a person, especially when you love them," she murmured.

Aaron reached out a hand and placed it on top of her left hand. "So, you were in love with him? I could always see it plainly on his face, but I couldn't get a read on you."

"I loved him so much, but we were never in love with each other."

Aaron's eyebrows rose as he pulled his hand back. "Now, that's a damn lie. I'm good at watching people. If Matt wasn't in love with you, I'd eat my hat."

She shrugged. "Are you sure you want to talk about Matt?"

"No, but it seemed like you need to."

That was perceptive. Hazel locked away her grief and changed the subject. "More truths?"

"Lay it on me."

She tipped her head back and stared up at the dark foliage above. "I don't want to marry you," she found herself saying. The words sounded way worse out loud than they did in her mind. She dropped her chin, expecting anger or embarrassment from Aaron, but all she saw was resignation and acceptance.

"I know, but our lots have been cast." His tone was bleak.

His words struck a chord inside her. "Are you being forced into this?" It was one thing for her to make a sacrifice—Harbor was her responsibility—but she wouldn't put it on someone else if they didn't want it.

He shook his head. "No, you misunderstood what I meant. We've both made decisions that have led us to this point. We can only move forward. Our choice has already been made." A small smile tugged at the corners of his mouth. "But on the positive side, after the blending, we'll leave everything behind and start fresh. Our life will be what we make it."

He made it sound so simple. "I'd like that."

"And..." he continued, "any preconceived notions I have of you, I'll try hard to toss out the window, if you'll do the same. This will be a learning process for the both of us."

"I'll do my best." She snagged the flask and took a healthy swig. The liquor burned all the way down to her belly. Hazel hissed through her teeth and set the spirits down, a bitter aftertaste in her mouth. "I don't know how you drink that. It's gross."

"I'll pretend you didn't say that," he said dryly. "But I'll keep in mind that you don't like moonshine." He clasped his hands in front of him and eyed her. "Are you attracted to me?"

She sputtered and then gaped at him. "Well, that was blunt."

"Yes."

"I'm not sure how you want me to answer that."

"Honestly."

Hazel bit the inside of her cheek as she gazed at Aaron. He was muscular like all the guys she'd grown up with, a product of hard labor. His square jaw was nice, but his eyes were a little too close to his large nose. He was nice looking, but she wasn't attracted to him.

"No."

"Oh, thank God," he mumbled. He flashed her a

quick smile. "I'm glad I'm not the only one."

"Am I ugly?" she asked slowly.

"No, but to me, you're plain."

That should have hurt her feelings, but she somehow found herself smiling. "Then we're on the same page." An idea took root in her mind. Who said they had to live their lives a certain way? They could live just as friends, partners. The idea calmed the churning in her belly. Hazel held her hand out for him to shake. "We can set our own rules. Why don't we live as roommates? Then you and I won't be forced into something we don't want."

Aaron's smiled faded to the serious mask he wore all the time. "Deal."

He clasped her hand, his rough calluses catching along her skin. Her brows furrowed as he turned their clasped hands and stared at the back of her hand.

"What's wrong?"

He flicked a glance up to her face and then back down to their hands. "You know that our arrangement can't be permanent. They'll expect us to produce the next heir, and soon."

Oh, how she knew. "True, but no one said *when* we have to."

"Do you really want to take the chance and wait?" he said, tracing one of her delicate blue veins.

Hazel eyed him hard. "You just said you agreed with me." Was he changing his mind already?

He lifted her hand and flipped it palm side up. "I do, but life in our world is short. If we wait too long, Harbor would be in danger."

Her breath stuttered as he dipped his head and pressed his lips to the inside of her wrist. A little flutter went through her chest. Well, that was uncomfortable. She tugged on her arm, and he relented, much to her relief.

He straightened and arched an eyebrow. "You're going to have to get used to me. I propose we try an experiment."

"And what's that?"

"A kiss."

Oh, boy.

CHAPTER EIGHT

Hazel

"A kiss," she repeated.

"A press of the lips, really."

Hazel bit her lip and nodded. "I guess we should try. It's better to know now if this will work."

She scooted a little closer, butterflies taking flight in her belly. Aaron shifted toward her, wrapped an arm around her waist and tugged her between his thighs. He brushed a blond strand away from her eyes and stared at her.

A nervous giggle escaped her. "This is awkward. Do you feel awkward? 'Cause I feel awkward."

"Take a deep breath. We can do this, Hazel."

"Okay," she whispered, watching him.

He kept his dark eyes open, slowly closed the distance between them, and touched his lips to hers. She watched him, noticing his dark lashes.

Aaron pulled back. "Anything?"

"It wasn't awful," she admitted. It wasn't really a kiss, more of a press of skin to skin.

"Let's see if we can do a little better."

He slid his hands up her arms, cupped her cheeks and kissed her a little harder this time. She jerked when his tongue traced her bottom lip. Again, it wasn't bad, but it was a little like kissing her brother. *Ew*. Her nose wrinkled. Now this was gross.

Hazel began to pull away when one hand slid into her hair and massaged her scalp. She melted. There wasn't anything she liked more than having her hair played with. He could kiss her as much as he wanted as long as he kept rubbing her scalp.

The world upended, startling her out of her scalp massaging haze. She blinked up at the night sky and the surrounding forest. How in the world had he moved them so easily? He kissed down her neck and made a move to return to her mouth.

"Aaron," she said, pushing at his chest. "It's not

working." Something dug into her spine as she wriggled beneath him. "There aren't any butterflies or anything, but that's okay. We don't really need passion to have children."

He slowly lifted his head. His cheeks were flushed, and his gaze narrowed. "Don't worry. I know all sorts of tricks. I'll have you panting as hard as me in no time."

"What?" she gasped, right before he bore down on her.

His teeth mashed against her lips brutally and he bit her, hard.

A cry burst from her and her head spun. That hurt. This was not what she'd signed up for, not at all. She tried to push him off of her, but he was too heavy. A spark of panic lit inside her as his hips settled between her legs.

"Stop!" she shouted, slapping at his shoulders. What was wrong with him?

He jerked his head up and Hazel took her opening and slapped him as hard as she could. She panted as he glared down at her. The air in her lungs froze at the dangerous glint in his eyes. It was part rage, part heat. "You're hurting me. Get off me!"

"So, you like it rough?" he growled low as he caught

her hands in one of his and held them tightly.

"No," she breathed, trying to wiggle out from underneath him. "That's not what I meant. Let me go. Everything will be alright, but you have to let me go."

"I can do rough," he said, ignoring her protest.

"Get off me!" she yelled, kicking her legs.

"I never imagined a girl like you would be into that sort of thing." He smiled, but it held a dark edge. "But I'm willing to try anything."

Her heart pounded fiercely in her chest as she began to thrash beneath him. "Let me go! Help!" His grip tightened painfully on her wrists, but she gritted her teeth and tugged harder. "Help me!" she screamed. She stared toward the firelight, but no one burst through the trees. No one came.

Aaron set his mouth near her ear. "It's okay. No one can hear you out here. Just let go and surrender. We'll figure this out together. Who knows? It might be fun. I've always wanted to try something like this. It will be sweeter knowing I'm your first."

She gagged and panted in fear. "Whatever this is, I don't want it. Do you understand me? I don't want it! Get the hell off of me!"

"Your mouth is saying no, but..." He pulled on her arms, forcing her body to arch into him. "But your body is telling me something different. Tonight is about being honest with each other. Let me help you be honest."

Nausea and terror filled her. She continued to buck and tried to free her hands. A scream caught in her throat when his free hand slid up her thigh and wedged between them. Desperate, she turned her head as his lips descended, looking for something, anything, to help her. It was impossible to reach her weapons, and no branch lay nearby. Hazel wailed, a sound thick with despair before the sight of his ear entered her vision. She opened her mouth and bared her teeth. Her papa had taught her to never go down without a fight. She darted forward and clamped down on his ear. Copper filled her mouth, but she held tight as he grunted and then yelled.

He stopped fumbling with her pants and tore free from her grasp. She never even saw the blow. Black dots danced across her eyes; pain radiated from the side of her face. Cold dirt pressed into her right cheek as she fought not to heave.

"Damn it, Hazel. Look at what you made me do."

Tears squeezed out of the sides of her eyes as he leaned down to kiss the side of her throbbing face. Bile burned the back of her throat. "You're a monster," she muttered.

"You started this and pushed me too far," he murmured. "I'm sorry. I didn't mean to hit you that hard." A finger traced her cheek, causing her to wince. "Why did you have to push me? I was trying to help you."

She cracked her watering eyes open and tried to focus on the wavering forest around her. "Get off of me," she croaked.

Large fingers grasped her chin and forced her to look up. His dark eyes had lost the crazy glint and now were unreadable. He scanned her face and tsked. "That's going to leave a bruise," he whispered. "It's a good thing the blending's tomorrow. We can figure this all out once we're married."

He was crazy if he thought she'd marry him after this, but wisely, she kept her mouth shut. She was alone, and at his mercy in the forest. But some of her thoughts must have been visible in her eyes, because his expression hardened.

"Now, listen here, Hazel. You've already accepted my proposal." He glanced to the side and then pinned her with a look. "When we leave here, you're going to act like your normal self."

"Like hell," she hissed.

Aaron cocked his head and leaned closer so that their noses touched. "Do you think they care about you? Those people at the party?"

She knew the answer. Only Baz and Mesa. She had to get to Baz and Mesa.

"No one will believe a word you say. Our peers like and trust me. When it comes down to both our stories tonight, who do you think they will believe?"

Him. They would stand behind him, but her family wouldn't. All she had to do was get home.

"Answer me," he whispered.

Hazel swallowed past the bile. "You."

If she plied him with what he wanted, he would release her. He had to. They had to go home at some point, and when they did, he was a dead man. Her brothers would make sure of it.

"That's right." He traced a finger over where he hit her. "Now, pull yourself together and we'll head back." She whimpered as he released her face and yanked her Glock from her thigh holster. "You can have this once we get back." He released her hands and stood up.

Hazel scrambled back, kicking, and lunged toward the bonfire. Her legs shook as leaves and branches slapped her in the face. She had to make it to Mesa and

Baz. The fire was so close. She stumbled and cried out when a hand wrapped around her waist and yanked her back into a hard chest.

"That is not pulling yourself together. You need to compose yourself." He propelled her forward and tucked her into his side. "Calm down."

They pushed through the trees and back into the writhing mass. People noticed their appearance and began whispering to each other. She searched the group for her friends, but they were nowhere to be found.

Jessy caught sight of them and swaggered to their side. "So, it's official?"

Aaron's arm tightened around her. "We're to be blended tomorrow."

Jessy whistled sharply, catching the attention of almost everyone. "Congratulations are in order. Our very own Aaron is to be blended with the founder's daughter."

Cheers and whistles rang out around them, but Hazel barely heard any of it. Tonight had started out as a dream, but turned into a nightmare. Colton smiled as he sauntered up to them, one girl on each arm. He shrugged both girls off and swept her into a hug.

"Congrats," he said.

"Where are my friends?" she whispered in his ear.

He pulled back, frowning, and cast a glance between her and Aaron. "They went home already," he said slowly.

"They left without me?" Her voice cracked. How could they leave her here? She shivered as Aaron hugged her to his side. Just his hands touching her made her want to puke everywhere. Each part of her felt dirty, defiled. And now her only chance to get home was to ride with him.

She sucked in a deep breath and pasted on a smile. All she had to do was fake it. Colton and Aaron were her ride home. She had to keep it together until she got home. Once she was home, she'd bring hell down on Aaron, but for now she needed to keep it together and let him assume he'd won.

Hazel let herself go numb, nodding at Aaron's friends when they came to congratulate them. The only thing memorable was the burning hate and jealousy on Gen's face when they connected eyes.

Aaron jiggled her, pulling her from her stare-off. She shuttered her gaze and peered up through her lashes. "What?"

He stared at her and then glanced around the

group. "It is well past my bride's bedtime." He spun them around and led her back toward the forest.

She dug her heels in. Oh, God. She couldn't go back

"You ready to break the news to your old man?" Colton's voice called from behind them.

Some of her panic faded with his voice. Aaron couldn't hurt her if there were witnesses. She curled her trembling fingers into fists and nodded her head yes. "He will be thrilled." The words tasted like ash on her tongue. Before tonight, yes, he would have. But after tonight, there was nowhere Aaron could hide that her papa and brothers couldn't find him. Perverse joy filled her. Justice would be served.

"Shotgun," she called when the Jeep came in view.

"As if," Jessy hollered, pushing past them and hopping into the front. "You get to sit with your betrothed."

She swallowed hard and forced herself not to look up at Aaron. At least Gen would sit between them. Her heart crashed to her feet when Gen took the outer right seat and Aaron tugged her toward the Jeep. He climbed in, pulling her with him.

Deep breaths. All she had to do was breathe deeply. The night from hell was almost over. She winced as his arm draped behind her. Her breath hitched in her throat. The arm currently lying on her skin felt like a cage. Colton started the Jeep and began rolling forward when she noticed something missing. "My bow! I left my bow!"

"I threw it in the back," Colton called.

Hazel nodded and kept her face averted from the monster at her side and stared out into the trees, watching them fade until their tires once again were on sand. This evening had taken a turn for the worst. She should've listened to her papa. Never again would she leave Harbor.

"Hey, Colton, you mind taking the long route home?"

"Sure."

She closed her eyes briefly, trying not to be sick. She could handle a ride.

You can do this.

"You're starting to worry me, Hazel. I thought we had made up," Aaron murmured near her ear. His hot breath caused a chill to run down her spine.

"Get out of my space," she muttered.

"What is yours is mine. Don't worry, everything will be better tomorrow. We'll get through this."

Her stomach flipped. There would be no tomorrow for them. She scooted as far away from him as possible without falling out of the Jeep. He laid his hand on her thigh and squeezed. Hazel wanted to slap it away and run, but there was nowhere to go.

Aaron sighed and leaned closer, his breath sweet and bitter. "You're making this difficult. Don't force my hand."

Heat built behind her eyes. He'd already forced too much.

"You know, your father and I speak often. About you specifically. He's raised concerns about you being fanciful and sometimes weak. I wonder what he will think when I bring you home high."

"What?" She whipped around and stared at Aaron with wide eyes. "What are you talking about?"

His face was a blank mask. "If you won't be reasonable, I will have to take things into my own hands."

She jerked as something pricked her leg. "Ouch." She hissed, swatting at his hand. He tossed something out of the Jeep as a little blood seeped out onto her jeans.

"What was that?" she asked.

"Something that will help you loosen up."

"You drugged me," she said flatly.

Jessy glanced between the two of them and then

burst into laughter. "What a classic way to end the night. She'll be so loose by the time we get home."

Hazel turned toward him and stared him down. "How does drugging you help me? My father will blame you for my condition, as will my brothers."

"No, they won't," Aaron said. "I'll be the man who protected you at a party you had no business attending. I will be the one who brought you home safely to your family after you drank too much."

Disgust filled her. "That's not true."

He shrugged. "That's not how I remember it." He turned to Gen. "Is that how you remember it?"

"Yep."

"Jessy?"

"You're the hero of this story."

"Colton?"

Her gaze caught his in the rearview mirror. Guilt flashed through his gaze before he dropped his eyes. "You've been a perfect gentleman all evening from what I've seen."

Betrayal seared her gut. She stared daggers at the back of Colton's head. Just when she thought he might be a normal human being. She knew better. "You coward," she hissed as his head wavered a moment and the road ahead of them seemed to tilt. "What did you give me?" she asked, placing a hand to her forehead.

"Something that will twist you up, so you can't remember up from down," Jessy chirped from the front seat. "No worries. You'll be right as rain tomorrow."

"You're all sad excuses for human beings," she hissed.

"Don't be like that," Aaron crooned.

He wavered, and she found herself grabbing for his shirt to steady herself. She snatched her hands back as soon as she realized what she'd done. Aaron grabbed them and held them tightly against his chest.

Hazel stared at him with all the disgust and loathing swirling inside her. "It doesn't matter what story you spin, I will never marry you. My father will *always* believe me. You think me being high will change your bloody outcome?" A hysterical laugh bubbled out of her. "You're a dead man walking."

He stayed silent and her wavering gaze slid to Gen's hand. It was perched on Aaron's shoulder, drawing a pattern along his neck. She didn't know why she fixated on the movement, but it struck her as odd after Aaron's comment earlier. If he didn't like her, why was he allowing her to caress him like a lover?

She glanced at him and stared resolutely back. He would pay.

He shook his head slowly at her, almost looking sad. "I was wrong about you, and so was your father. You're just like your mother. Too much like her."

"How do you know about my mother?" she asked, her words garbled.

"Goodbye, Hazel."

"Wha...?" Her breath whooshed out when he shoved a hard hand against her chest.

For one breathless moment, she was airborne, her gaze locked with Aaron's. He didn't blink, and neither did she. Shock, anger, and betrayal passed between them in that moment. Time sped up and one long screech was all she emitted before her body collided with the ground. The impact had her gasping for breath that wouldn't come. Nor could she scream from the acute pain that crashed into her, wave after wave, as she skidded across the desert floor.

Abruptly, her body slammed into something, stopping her tumbling. She wheezed as tears squeezed out of the corners of her eyes, her lungs screaming for air. Panic had her trying to sit up, only to slam back to the rough sand when the world spun around her.

The sky swirled and then darkened as one last thought went through her mind.

It wasn't the Tainted she needed to be worried about; it was the human monsters.

CHAPTER NINE

Hazel

Hazel's fingers twitched near her sides, brushing the gritty surface beneath her. Sand? Well, that was peculiar. Why was there sand in her bed?

She cracked her eyes open and immediately regretted it. A groan slipped from her mouth as pain slammed into her. The stars above her swirled and her head pounded in sync with her galloping heart. Stars? Where the hell was she?

A flash of Aaron passed through her mind. Her breath seized. That bastard had pushed her from the Jeep—a moving vehicle.

Hazel jerked up into a sitting position only to slam back to the ground as agony assaulted her. Stones bit into her back, but that was the least of her pain. Her right hand fluttered over her ribs and the hot skin of her left arm. Heat radiated from her forearm, along with pulses of pain. That sure felt like a broken arm.

Gritting her teeth, she gently pressed against the tender flesh. Stars flashed across her vision and her stomach rolled. She turned her throbbing head just in time to spill the contents of her stomach. Bile burned the back of her throat and inside her nose, causing her eyes to water. She squeezed her eyes closed and panted, trying to work through the pain.

Aaron tried to kill her, and no one had said a thing. Sick and wrong. It was one thing to bully someone, but another thing to stand aside when they drugged you and attempted to kill you.

Slowly, she turned her head away from the contents of her stomach and weakly wiped her mouth with the back of her right hand. She held her hand up to the moonlight and squinted at the damaged flesh. It looked like her hand had been run through a meat grinder, everything raw and bleeding. She'd helped their doctors in Harbor, so blood and wounds weren't unfamiliar, but there was something about it being her body that made the world waver around her.

She snapped her eyes shut and attempted to slow her breathing. *You cannot pass out, Hazel Bresh. If you pass out, you're vulnerable.*

With care, Hazel placed her hand by her side and hissed when pain rocked her body just from that little movement. She stared up at the night sky as the force of her predicament slapped her in the face. She was in the wilderness. By herself. Without her weapons. Her heart sped up as fear began to trickle into her veins. *One thing at a time, Hazel. Do not panic.*

First, she needed to discover her location. She'd never been out here, so that would make it difficult. Was it possible she'd only passed out for a moment? She desperately scanned the area around her in hopes of seeing taillights. Her heart sank.

No sign of the Jeep. Or any humans. Nothing but moonlit desert on one side and a darkened forest on the other. But that was okay. She'd follow the Jeep tracks in the morning. Her gaze darted to the tree line and a shiver worked down her spine as she stared at the deeply shadowed woods. Aaron was the least of her worries right now. If her injuries didn't kill her, the Tainted that lurked out here would. Terror seized her as her brothers' stories of monsters filtered through her memory.

Unnatural. Disfigured and deadly. Nightmares in the flesh.

A sob built in her chest as the dark shadows between the trees began to form monsters.

She would die. It was only a matter of time.

Tears tracked down her cheeks in wet rivulets, her body trembling as the cool ground seeped into the back of her torn shirt. Another sob bubbled up, but she stifled it. Hazel squinted at the unmoving sinister shapes, her bottom lip quivering. One lifted its arm and waved at her. She blinked and stifled the hysterical laugh threatening to slip past her lips. A damn branch.

They're not real monsters. It's just your imagination, and you're in shock. Calm down. You need to get out of here before real monsters arrive.

Hazel pulled in a shuddering breath and exhaled softly. She couldn't panic or let fear rule her. If she did, she'd die. Her brows furrowed as she went over the training her brothers had drilled into her over the years. She needed to assess her injuries, acquire a weapon, and find high ground. The rest would have to wait until the morning.

If she made it until morning.

Her breath rushed out as her eyes darted around. She'd already been exposed for too long. It was a bloody miracle nothing had picked her off yet. Her pulse picked up and she had to remind herself to breathe steadily. There was no time to panic. Each moment she dallied was one closer to death.

Muscle by muscle, she forced herself to relax and then began her examination.

"Damn it," she breathed as she probed her ribs. Bruised to hell, but at least none were broken like her arm. Climbing with broken ribs would be nearly impossible. Next, she shifted her legs and toes. That hurt but brought a smile to her face. At least she could move them. That meant her spine wasn't damaged.

Something rustled behind her and she froze. The hair on her arms rose when the rustling stopped and silence descended. Hazel held her breath and cocked her head toward the sound.

Nothing—nothing that she could see, anyway.

Never taking her eyes away from the trees, she slid her hand toward a rock by her side. Her fingers curled around the stone and she waited. Every creak from the trees had her on edge. Five minutes passed, and then ten, but nothing stirred or rustled.

She was injured prey, an easy target. If there was

something hunting her, surely it would have pounced already. That was enough to push her into continuing her examination.

Hazel kept her eyes on the forest, forced her fingers to release her death hold on the rock at her side, and began to gingerly run her hand over her face. She nearly yelped when her fingers pressed into an oozing wound near her right temple. A curse slipped from her lips as her fingers came away wet. She wouldn't bleed to death, but that much blood would draw every Tainted within a half mile in her direction. Her pulse picked up pace. She had to get out of here. Now.

She ran her tongue along her busted bottom lip, and then along the swollen ridge of the inside of her cheek. She'd taken a chunk out of her cheek and bitten her lip at some point, but all her teeth were still intact. Her gaze wandered to her limp left arm and then back to the trees. She'd survive her injuries, provided there wasn't any internal damage.

Time to go. She clutched at her jeans with her good hand. This would hurt. A grunt escaped through her clenched teeth as she struggled to sit up. She clamped her lips closed against the cry struggling to get out. The world spun, forcing her to release her grip on her jeans and steady herself. Her jagged nails dug into the sand and sweat beaded on her brow. She was upright, but the worst was yet to come.

Cracking her eyes, she scanned the ground and smiled grimly at the small stick lying within reach. She plucked in from the ground and placed it between her teeth, ignoring the crunch of grit. Rubbing the bottom of her tank-top between her fingers, she steeled herself against her next task. As carefully as possible, she wedged her hand underneath her left forearm. Tears sprang to her eyes and her stomach churned with the pain, but she swallowed hard and lifted her left arm.

A bellowing cry burst from her throat as she placed her arm across the bottom of her shirt and straightened the bone pressing against her skin unnaturally. Colors danced across her vision and drool dripped down her chin as pain threatened to drown her. Horrendous. If a Tainted beast attacked her at that moment, she would've welcomed it with wide arms to get rid of the terrible pain. She dry-heaved and panted as the acute pain receded to a persistent throb, but it was mild enough that she could grab the edge of her torn tank-top. Now, time to create a sling.

She whimpered when she lifted the edge and tied it to her left strap with the help of her teeth. Tears dripped down her face and weariness settled over her as the cool air brushed against her exposed midriff. What she wouldn't do for a nap. Her eyelids lowered, and her head dropped as if her neck wasn't strong enough to hold it up. Not a good sign. She needed the adrenaline to keep her going and could not afford it to wane.

A lone howl tore through the air.

Ice seemed to leach into her veins and her eyes snapped open, all traces of sleepiness disappearing.

"Stars above," she whispered through numb lips. The hunt had begun.

She forced herself to stand on wobbly legs and lurched toward the forest. Terror like no other squeezed her heart. Who knew what kind of beast it was ... but whatever it was, it sounded big and hungry.

Her sandal snapped, causing her to stumble and almost lose her footing. Of all the days to wear sandals. Hazel kicked both shoes off and half ran, half stumbled, toward the shadows. She didn't need shoes to run.

Another howl rent the air.

Her breath seized, and she changed directions. It

sounded so much closer, and it had come from a different direction. Panic twisted in her gut. Were there two? Or was the Tainted moving that quickly? Was it possible she was running straight toward it?

She didn't have time to second-guess herself. The desert offered no shelter or protection. She entered the tree line and had to force herself to keep moving into the darkness. Practically blind, she tripped and stumbled but managed to keep upright. She squinted at the trees, and her panic doubled. She couldn't climb any of them. The branches were too far apart—impossible for someone with only one arm to climb.

Hazel forced herself to keep moving. Each wasted second put her in more danger. She swung around a large tree and almost shouted with relief. A huge tree loomed ahead of her with a branch low enough that she could pull herself up. She started for it when a howl pierced the silence, followed by three answering calls echoing in her ears.

Fear had her scrambling up the tree. White flashed across her vision as she jarred her arm in the mad climb, the rough bark tearing at her bare feet and hands. A small cry escaped her when her foot slipped. Hazel gritted her teeth and dug her toes into a little notch on the tree trunk. She wrapped her arm around the branch and pushed up with all her might. Her breath stuttered when her torso slammed into the branch, her ribs screaming. A snarl had her jerking her legs up just as something snapped its teeth below her.

She balked when she locked eyes with a black-eyed, tainted beast. *A lobo*. Originally, it might have been a coyote, but it was now bigger than any wolf she'd ever read about. It growled, its lips pulling back over its teeth. That's the only warning she received before it lunged again. Hazel jerked back, wobbling precariously over the branch as its teeth snapped beneath where her face had been. She grabbed the branch above and heaved while turning, so that she sat on the branch with her feet pulled up. Her whole body trembled as she tucked her feet underneath her and forced herself to climb higher into the tree. One mistake and she was toast.

Three more beasts burst from the foliage and she froze. She hadn't even heard them approach. That wasn't good. Lobos were usually solitary creatures unless they were teaching their pups to hunt. One lobo was survivable, but three? A shiver worked through her as she climbed higher, each movement calculated and precise. It was hard to keep her eyes from the snarling monsters below her. Every time she looked away from them, it felt like she was tempting fate. Hazel screamed when the largest beast ran at the tree and used the trunk as a springboard. Its paws scrabbled at the branch before it slipped and fell back to the ground.

They're trying to climb the tree.

She clutched at the tree as it swayed, her eyes wide. It had jumped at least ten feet. Not only were they vicious, but they were smart. That did not bode well for her. She reached for the next branch and made to stand when her foot slipped. Her mouth opened, but no sound escaped as she fell. She slammed into the tree trunk and screamed as her arm caught between branches. A broken arm was nothing compared to the searing pain shooting down her shoulder and arm. Blinking through her tears, she placed her feet on the first branch she could and locked her legs. Her whole body shook as she pulled her arm from the branches. There was no way she could climb any higher now. She'd pass out and fall from the tree. Hazel wedged herself into a tangle of branches and wrapped herself around the tree limbs.

Blood dripped down her good arm in a constant stream. The dark concealed much of her wound, but she knew it was bad. She needed to stop the bleeding, but all she had were leaves and her jeans.

Hazel snagged a few large leaves from the branches and used her finger tips of her broken arm to set them on the massive gash running down her right arm. It wasn't much, but it would have to do.

Her arms and legs flashed hot and then cold. The world around her warped and spun. Her cheeks met the rough bark as she fought the dizziness that was as dangerous as the beasts below her. What she wouldn't give for a length of rope. The growls below her were enough of a reminder to keep her fighting the pain. All she had to do was make it through the night.

One of the Tainted let loose a snarl that would surely haunt her dreams.

It would be a long night. Hopefully, her blood wouldn't call anymore beasties.

CHAPTER TEN

Hazel

A day and a half passed. Despite all odds, she'd survived two nights in the wilds, but her time was coming to an end. The tree had been her salvation, but it had also become her prison.

"Stupid animals," she whispered through cracked lips, glaring down at the lobos that hadn't ceased their circling. They had been snapping and growling for hours. The largest paused and tilted its snout up at her, growling. "Yeah, yeah, I don't like you that much either."

Everything hurt. Even her hair hurt. She didn't even know that was possible. Her main problem wasn't the broken arm or … she glanced at the jagged gash that ran from her shoulder to forearm; it still wept blood, despite her leafy bandages. She needed stitches, but more so—water. Hazel rolled her head to the side and swallowed against her dry throat. The more she dwelled on it, the thirstier she became.

Closing her eyes, she rested her cheek against the rough bark. Sleep was the answer. The pain, hunger, fear, and thirst all disappeared when she slept. But her mind didn't shut down. It wandered toward a subject she hadn't let herself dwell on—her family.

What were they doing right now? Were they searching for her? A pang of guilt stabbed her. If only she'd said no to Aaron and gone home. She'd let her emotions decide instead of her mind. It was utterly stupid, and she knew better. Her heart squeezed. Her brothers would mourn her, but it would kill her poor papa. He was hard on her and sheltered her, but it was because he loved her. Her eyes stung, but no tears came. Now she'd never see them again, and that was on her.

The idea of never having her brothers steal food from the counter when she was cooking, or her papa draping blankets over them when they fell asleep on the couch, or sitting around a fire to celebrate a good day of hard work, about broke her.

A spark of anger burned in her gut, dissolving some of her numbness. Taking responsibility for her actions was a bitter pill to swallow, but the deceit and betrayal of Aaron, Colton, and Gen cut deep. Part of her wanted to rant and scream at the world for what they'd done, but frankly, she didn't have the energy for it.

Another snarl brought her back to herself. Hazel glanced down at the largest of the wolves and bared her teeth. "Oh, shut up! I'm sick and tired of hearing all of your racket. Go find your meal somewhere else!"

Its pointed ears laid back against its skull, never losing eye contact.

"Get out of here," she growled down at it.

The lobos snarled at her challenge but didn't budge. They stared at each other for what seemed like forever. Hazel itched to blink, but she didn't dare. She wouldn't be marked as weak. Even in her dire circumstances, she found beauty in the situation. The beast's fur was wine-colored, with a light terracotta striped pattern, similar to that of a tiger she'd read about once. She'd never seen one this close before. What had caused that genetic mutation? Tigers weren't found in the old United States unless it escaped from a zoo.

She blinked when the beast shook its head and snarled at her one last time before darting into the trees. She frowned. What had caused that response? Was it because she didn't back down? Doubtful. The two other beasts' ears perked up, and soon followed out of sight. Odd. What would have scared them off? She shuddered, the answer clear. Larger predators.

Fear ran down her spine. If it scared the pack off of their prey, it must be something fearsome. With slow, careful movements she lifted her head and surveyed the surrounding area. Nothing stirred. She held still and listened to the surrounding forest. No birds chirped. It was as if the forest held its breath.

Sweat beaded at her nape and she placed her cheek against the tree, trying to blend in. Whatever lurked out there was dangerous enough that the whole forest wanted to escape its notice. She couldn't afford to attract its attention. Minutes trickled by and her skin pebbled in the silence. Each breath seemed too loud.

She jerked, and a scream caught in her throat when a bird cawed, shattering the quiet. Her pulse galloped, but she kept still. In increments, the forest sounds resumed, and her racing heart slowed. Whatever the danger had been, it had passed. This was her chance to escape.

But her body didn't want to move.

Hazel turned her face toward the tree and pressed her forehead against it. She needed to move, but the task ahead felt like too much. How was she to climb down without the use of her arms? Her gaze slid down. It had to be close to twenty feet to the ground. It wasn't possible to jump from that high. Helplessness washed over her.

If she stayed here, she died. If she slipped while climbing down, she died. If she stumbled across a predator, she died. Every path led to her death.

"Stop it," she growled at herself. "You're not weak. This is challenging, but it's not impossible."

Nothing was impossible. If she set her mind to it, she could do it.

She eyed the distance to the ground and the surrounding branches. If she moved slowly and chose her path with care, she could do it. Painfully. Her father didn't believe she had the grit her mother did. Time to prove him wrong.

She swung her leg over the branch and her calf cramped. She hissed out a curse and flexed her left foot repeatedly. Once the pain eased, she did the same to her right foot just in case. If her leg cramped on the way down, it would kill her or leave her maimed.

Hazel scrutinized the branches below and spotted her first destination. Three branches formed a V, with one branch shooting through the middle. If she placed a foot on each of the outside branches, leaned against the tree and lowered herself, she could sit on the middle one once she was low enough.

Her eyes moved to her thighs. Hopefully, she still had enough strength to do it. "Here goes nothing," she muttered.

Getting her feet on the branches was easy enough, but sinking into a squat without falling proved to be a challenge.

A squeak escaped her when her legs collapsed. Her butt slammed into the branch below her; pain shot up her spine and down her spread legs, but she didn't fall. That was a success in her book.

"You're okay, Hazel," she muttered, ignoring her stinging back. From the feel of it, the bark had scraped her right through her shirt. "You only fell a few inches. If you can do that a few more times, you'll be at the bottom in no time."

Every movement was painful, and slow-going, but she made it to the last branch. It wasn't too far from the ground, but far enough that, without the use of her arms, it would hurt. She debated her options before settling on rolling onto her stomach. No matter what, the jump would jar her arms, but if she slid off the branch backwards, there was less chance of her falling forward and onto her face and broken arm.

Her elbow bumped into the branch as she twisted. White-hot pain flashed across her vision. "Damn it," she panted through the pain, eyes squeezed shut. She really needed a better sling. The pain ebbed, allowing her to take one moment to gather her courage. "You can do this," she whispered and wiggled backward. Gravity then took care of the rest.

For a long moment, she was weightless. Then, the moment passed, and her bare feet slammed against the ground. Shooting pain raced through the arches of her feet and up her legs. Her knees buckled, and she crashed onto her butt, pain attacking her abused body from all sides, but she welcomed it. With watering eyes, she glanced up at the tree. She'd made it down. Survived. She did it.

"I did it," she said as emotion clogged her throat. "I did it."

"Did what, darling?" a rusty male voice drawled.

Her body locked up. Her gaze scoured the surrounding trees, but she couldn't spot the source of the voice. Only fiends and criminals hid who they were. Time to get out of here.

"Who are you?" she asked, pulling her feet underneath her and sloppily pushing herself upright. The world tilted; she stumbled a few steps. Stars above, that wasn't good.

"Looks like you could use a little help." The voice had come from her right. She clenched her hand into a fist, blood squishing from between her fingers.

"Are you offering?" she asked, facing where she'd heard the voice, and pretended to stumble backward. The wilds were dangerous. It wasn't only the Tainted you had to look out for, but also the depraved humans who had survived the apocalypse. Let him think she was weaker than she was. That might give her the advantage.

"You here alone?" he crooned.

Alarm bells rang in her mind. Whoever this guy was, he wasn't a friend. "Nope," she said, drunkenly weaving toward the left side of the tree.

"That's too bad. And here, I thought we could play."

Adrenaline flooded her. She lunged forward and sprinted away from the tree. A shout rent the air, but she didn't turn to look. Her legs quivered, and dizziness assaulted her, but it wasn't enough to slow her down. Her head start was the only thing she had going for her. Desperately, she searched the trees around her for a hiding space. Fatigue rode her hard. Too much time without food and water had taken its toll. Branches slapped her in the face as she pushed through foliage, tearing at her skin. Just a little further.

A hand closed around her right arm, yanking her to a stop. A scream exploded out of her. Agony. Blinding agony. She kicked at her assailant. "Let go," she cried. "Please, let go."

He didn't. Her agony doubled when he shook her like a ragdoll, fingers digging into her wound. "Stop screaming."

She whimpered, trying to sort through the spinning images around her. But she couldn't tell where her agony ended and she began. All she knew was pain. Heat suffused her back; a hand slid along her shoulder and wrapped around her neck, forcing her chin up.

"What do we have here?" a nasally voice crooned.

If only he'd let go of her arm…

"A morsel," the first voice answered.

Her heart thumped against her chest. Two men, not one. "Let me go," she croaked.

"It appears to be damaged."

"Never stopped me."

Hazel forced her eyes open, and horror couldn't even begin to describe the feeling coiling inside her. Fear unlike anything she'd ever known caused her pulse to jackknife. *A Tainted.* A nightmare in the flesh. A monster.

The Tainted male glanced down at her and smiled, his yellow rotten teeth all on display. "See something you like?"

Terror. Horror. Disgust. She thought she knew the meaning of Tainted. She'd expected a monster, a rabid animal that walked like a man, but never imagined anything like this. Unable to tear her eyes away, she stared up at where his nose should have been. Instead, there was a snout, like a pig. Bile burned the back of her throat and she gagged. It was like part of his face was made of melted wax, a grotesque combination of both human and swine. *Monstrous.*

His beady eyes narrowed. "You think you're too good for the likes of me?" he asked, shaking her roughly. "You take it, Blade." He shoved her away.

The Tainted had names and spoke? She stumbled and caught her foot on a rock. The earth rushed to meet her, and she braced for the pain. But there was no way to prepare for the pain. Fire raced through her body, short-circuiting her brain. It was the sort of pain that could make someone insane. After everything she'd been through in the last several days, she didn't know it was possible to hurt so much. "Please," she sobbed. "Please, make it stop."

But it didn't. Her arms stayed pinned beneath her body as boots kicked her legs open. A hand grabbed her ponytail and jerked back.

"Stop screaming, wench, or I'll kill ya," the rusty voice threatened behind her.

Was that the sound she kept hearing?

"Gag her, Will, or she'll bring the whole forest down on us."

Hazel forced her eyes open, the pig man coming into view. "Please, help me," she cried. "My arms."

His smile turned cruel, wrinkling his distorted face in a way that turned her stomach. His fingers clenched around the filthy bandana in his palm as he dropped into a squat by her face. "You should have chosen me."

She snapped her mouth shut against the screams that fought to escape when he reached forward. No way was he gagging her.

He shook his head at her and pinched her nose closed. Her breath burned in her lungs. Once she exhaled, he'd have her. The Tainted behind her yanked her hair, causing her to cry out. That's when the pig man wrestled the smelly fabric between her lips and tied it behind her head as the other Tainted settled between her legs.

"No," she cried. Had she survived Aaron only to endure this torture?

He leaned closer, his foul breath washing over her. "If you thought I was ugly, you don't even want to know what's between your legs now." Tears tracked down her face as he brushed a blunt finger along her cheek. "Such perfection. I haven't seen one of you in a long time." He smiled and pressed a dirty nail into the gash at her shoulder. Her vision dipped and darkened as her pain increased.

"That's right," he whispered. "Scream. We live for them." He licked his lips. "I can't wait to taste your sweet flesh. I reckon it will be the best meal I've had in a long time."

Somewhere in the recesses of her mind it clicked. She dry-heaved, bile dripping around the bandana and down her chin. After they'd used her, they'd eat her. He might look part human, but he was truly a monster.

A male bellow sounded behind her and the hand in her hair disappeared. A weight collapsed on her legs, pinning her. Hazel's eyes snapped open when something warm sprayed across her face. The Tainted gaped at her with an arrow protruding from his shoulder. His eyes rolled back into his head and his snout face-planted into the ground next to hers.

Help? She peeked up from underneath her wet lashes and hope fluttered in her chest. A young woman advanced toward them, her green hood up. She crouched next to the pig man and pushed back her hood. The knot of fear in her chest loosened some. Black hair with one red stripe slipped from a loose braid that framed her face. A normal face.

"Help," she said, the bandana muffling her words.

The girl's gaze flickered to her and held. Her body flashed hot and cold. A muffled gasp slipped from her when the girl's pupils expanded. Vertically-slitted pupils.

Tainted.

Darkness encroached on her vision as the monster reached for her.

CHAPTER ELEVEN

Hazel

Hazel awoke to a flash of intense pain. Tears dripped out of her eyes as she squinted up at the girl laying her arm beside her.

Not a girl. A Tainted.

She kicked out at the monster, landing a blow on her stomach. The Tainted tumbled backward as Hazel jerked into a sitting position and scrambled to her feet. She steadied herself against the tree and backed away as the Tainted glared at her from the ground.

Her brows slashed together, and she glanced at her arm, the one currently grasping the tree, then back to the now-standing Tainted. Her arm had been bandaged, but why? Without taking her eyes from the Tainted scrutinizing her, she pulled her brother's knife from the sheath at her waist. Her arm shook as she held it out in front of her.

"Stay back," she said, and retreated a step.

The Tainted arched a black brow. "And what do you think you're going to do with that little blade?"

"Come closer and find out," she croaked, and cleared her stinging throat. Nothing like that had ever come out of her mouth, but she was done pussyfooting around. Her blade wasn't ideal, but she could wield it, and *no one* would hurt her again.

"I could take that from you, but I'll let you keep it for now. We all need the appearance of safety, especially after..." She kicked the hairy monster in the side. "These monsters got a hold of you. Not that you deserved it."

A hysterical laugh burst out of her. They were all monsters. "So says the monster," she whispered.

Snake-like eyes clashed with hers, a vertical pupil surrounded by an unnatural emerald green. "I wouldn't cast stones." Disgust crossed the Tainted's face. "You're more monstrous than I am."

Hazel shuddered and took another step back.

The Tainted cocked her head. "What? No

comment?"

She eyed the Tainted, not knowing what to say.

The snake girl scoffed. "Of course, you wouldn't defend yourself. You know the truth." She sighed. "I can't let you leave. You're too dangerous."

Hazel snorted. The conversation was getting weirder by the moment. Anyone could see she was as weak as a lamb. There wasn't anything dangerous about her. Her muscles seized when the snake girl smoothly pulled her bow from her shoulder and nocked an arrow. Absently, Hazel admired how nice the bow was. The wood was well-oiled and practically shone. It was another thing those traitors had taken from her. She'd add it to the long list of grievances she carried in her heart.

Another laugh threatened to break loose. Something was wrong with her. She had an arrow aimed at her heart and she was thinking about bows. Swallowing down her hysteria, she took another slow step. Fear would not stop her from escape.

She winced when the Tainted's eyes narrowed. Stars above, that was creepy.

"Stop right there," the girl commanded.

Yeah, right. She'd rather get shot than comply. Whatever the Tainted had in store for her wouldn't be pleasant. A stick cracked underneath her bare heel and a familiar sound slapped her in the face.

A rattle.

She stilled, eyes wide. Part of her wanted to search the ground for the familiar beastie, but she knew she wouldn't spot it before it struck. Being struck by a rattlesnake was a death sentence. A painful one. The virus was only passed from bites and bodily fluids these days.

Rule number one: never get bitten.

"Make my death quick," she whispered. If she survived the bite and mutation, she didn't want to live her life as a monster. Hazel closed her eyes and waited for the pain, surprisingly calm. The air whistled, and she heard a dull thwack.

"It's dead."

Cracking one eye, she stared at the Tainted, not sure whether she believed her. Hazel eyed her with distrust but went over the facts. The Tainted had saved her from—her eyes dipped to the monsters on the ground—those things, and she'd fixed Hazel's dislocated arms. Obviously, she wanted her alive.

Twisting to the side, she searched the surrounding ground. "Stars above," she breathed when she spotted the rattler. Part of its body underneath a rock, the exposed half bent back on itself. She blinked at the arrow passed right through its skull, nailing it to the ground. If it wasn't for the arrow, she wouldn't have been able to spot it at all. Her lip curled back as she glared down at the serpent. The mutation gave the beasties an unfair advantage that led to so many deaths.

Something stung her arm. Hazel whipped around and pulled a dart from her arm. Her eyelids dropped, and her legs dropped out from under her. Arms caught her and lowered her to the ground. She glared at the Tainted above her. That sneaky wench.

"You drugged me," she slurred.

The Tainted smirked at her. "You gave me no other choice. I won't lie and say I didn't enjoy it after you kicked me in the chest."

"Well, that's petty."

Hazel gasped and cringed back when the Tainted grinned at her and flashed pointy fangs.

The Tainted's smile dropped and her expression hardened. "You're all the same. I won't feel bad about what comes next."

"Next?" Hazel forced out through numb lips as the world took on a dream-like quality.

"This was your choice. It will get worse before it

gets better."

Pain was her new reality.

Whatever the Tainted had knocked her out with still burned.

She glared at the Tainted's back. They'd been walking for three days.

Three days ago, she'd woken with the worst headache of her life with all her wounds cleaned and bandaged. What surprised her was that the Tainted had left her with her dagger. When the Tainted noticed her attention, she'd held out a dart, wiggled it, and smiled. The threat was clear. If Hazel attacked her, she'd get darted.

She didn't attack, she ran.

But that didn't work out so great either. Her captor had overtaken her in a matter of seconds. She was fast. Faster than she ought to have been. Well, compared to a human.

Her punishment had been swift and painful. The fabric that had been wrapped around her feet as makeshift shoes were retracted. It wasn't horrible in the forest, but once they hit the sand and rock, it *burned*.

Hazel cast a sullen glance in the Tainted's direction

and then down to her feet. Her abused body wanted nothing more than to collapse against the earth. They'd started up the side of a mountain this morning and she'd slipped twice already. It was only by the continued threats that she kept on.

Thankfully, her prickly captor didn't make her walk through the night. Every night, the snake girl held a dart up as a reminder, not that Hazel needed it. Sleep claimed her almost immediately ... except for last night.

She had almost been asleep when the Tainted jerked to a stand to scan the area. "Stay here," she'd commanded, and disappeared into the darkness. Hazel had been on full alert, straining to hear movement around her. Had the girl left her on her own? This was her chance. On quiet feet, she'd stood and crept away from their camp spot.

A deep growl had rumbled from behind her. Ever so slowly, she had peeked over her shoulder. Nothing. There was absolutely nothing there. Her shoulders had sagged. She must have been imagining it. She'd taken one step when it struck. There hadn't been any time to scream, run, or even lift her arms up, so she'd closed her eyes and waited for death.

It didn't come.

A slick hiss followed by a thwack and a growl caused her eyes to pop open. She locked eyes with a golden-eyed feline. It growled low, a mournful sound, before stilling. Her body had trembled from head to toe. She scrambled back, never looking away from the dead creature. Her captor had prowled out of the dark and dropped to her knees to yank out the arrow.

"What is it?" she'd asked through chattering teeth.

"A diablo."

"A devil?" she'd murmured through numb lips. It was huge.

"Yes, because it's a devil of a time killing them."

She eyed the patterned fur. It was a series of dark red-brown spots inside lighter spots. It blended in perfectly with its surroundings. No wonder it had been impossible to see. "How did you know it was there?"

"I didn't, but it's been trailing me since I picked you up. I knew it would show itself if there was an opportunity."

By opportunity, she meant ... her stomach rolled. "You used me as bait."

"You smell like blood. Plus, you left bloody scraps of fabric for it to follow. It wanted you, not me. Now, we can continue on without looking over our shoulders." Her captor had paused, giving her a puzzled look. "She *hesitated."*

"The beast?"

"Yeah, she faltered as if she couldn't track you. If it hadn't been for that, things could've turned out a lot differently."

She stumbled and latched onto the sagebrush to keep from falling. The sick feeling hadn't left her. Her breath came in hard pants as she stared down at the shale-covered earth.

"You're slowing us down."

Her teeth gnashed together. "If I had my shoes, maybe I wouldn't."

Something rustled and her makeshift shoes landed at her feet.

"Put them on. We're wasting time."

"Then just leave me," she growled. That's all she really wanted.

"I don't think so. Move, or I'll make you move."

Hazel scowled at the Tainted's back as she tried to brush the sand off her feet, but only managed to smear it with the blood. She gave up and slipped her make-shift moccasins on. Bliss. She sighed as the leather encased her torn feet. With one last glare at the Tainted, she continued to climb. Between failed escape attempts, she'd badgered the girl constantly about why she was taking her and where they were going. The only answer she received was that she was valuable.

Frustration had her fingers curling into fists. Each step took her further away from Harbor and her family. A warm breeze ruffled her hair, and she turned her face toward it. Standing on top of Harbor's wall was exhilarating, but it didn't compare to the view the mountainside offered. From this high, she could see the entire valley. She squinted, just barely making out a corner of Harbor. Her heart sank. Her home wavered. It seemed so close, and yet so far. One fat tear slipped out of her eye and plopped onto the dry ground. She'd been holding on to the hope she could make it home. But there were miles of wilds and Tainted between her and home. Even if she escaped, something would kill her along the way back. She needed to heal, needed supplies and weapons. None were within her grasp.

"Pining for your hellhole?"

Helplessness and fear of her future caused her to snap. "What is your problem?" Hazel swung back around. "What have I ever done to you?"

The Tainted planted her hands on her hips. "You exist and that's enough."

It was some sort of prejudice, then. "If my existence offends you, let me go. I don't like you, you don't like me. The simple solution is to free me."

"You're free. Are you in chains?"

Hazel stared. "I may not be wearing physical chains, but they're there all the same. Every time I run, you drag me back."

"I do what I must."

"And what's that?" She held her breath. Maybe she'd answer this time.

"My duty to my people."

"Your people have tasked you to kidnap and torture innocent people?"

Something flashed across her captor's face before it disappeared. It resembled guilt.

"You know nothing about duty and honor."

"That's where you're wrong. I know everything about duty, honor, and the meaning of sacrifice." Did she ever. She studied the Tainted girl. Her posture screamed aggression. Time to try a different tactic. "I think we might have more in common than you think."

"We are nothing alike. You destroy, kill, and maim. I heal, defend, and protect."

Hazel frowned. Her captor's words were biting and

bitter. They reeked of pain. "Has someone like me hurt you before?" she asked softly. Pain and bitterness were her constant companions these days. That was something she could understand and empathize with.

Silence.

"I promise, I'm nothing like the person you described. Please let me go. Help me."

"I've helped you," the Tainted said woodenly.

Well, she'd bandaged her to continue her torture. "I thank you for taking care of my wounds, but you and I both know you didn't do it to help me."

Her captor shifted and glanced away. "I've also clothed and fed you, not that you've been grateful." Her alien gaze skittered back to Hazel and away. "You'd feel better if you ate something."

Hunger gnawed at her stomach. Her captor offered her meat every day and Hazel always declined, despite her hollow belly. *Rule number two: never eat tainted meat.* She'd get infected if she did. She'd resorted to eating cactus that looked normal-ish, but it wasn't enough to hold her. She needed protein, and soon. As for the clothing… "You took my shoes away," she said flatly. "My feet are still bleeding." They throbbed with her words.

"Because you were trying to run away!" Color

rushed into her captor's bronzed cheeks.

Because she had kidnapped her. Hazel kept those thoughts locked inside. "Please, just let me go," she pleaded. "You need never to tell your people you even found me."

Her captor's mouth pressed into a thin line. "I've told you before, you're too dangerous and too valuable to let escape. Stop playing the innocent."

Hazel barked out a laugh and gestured to her body. "Do I look dangerous to you?"

Snake eyes settled on her face. "That's what makes you such a threat. You're the enemy."

"That's the first truthful thing to come out of your mouth in three days," Hazel said.

The Tainted turned on her heel and marched up the mountain without answering.

"Wench."

"Hurry up, or I'll drag you by your hair," the Tainted called.

She forced her legs to move and continued the climb from hell. An evil smile spread across her face as she thought about what was hidden away in her empty leg holster. It had taken some finagling, but she'd managed to steal one of the darts that her captor was so fond of using. When the moment was right, she'd use it.

She amused herself by imagining the look on the Tainted's face when she darted her. Maybe she was as demented as the Tainted accused her of. Her brows slashed together at the thought occurring to her.

"Hey," she called, a little breathless, her lungs burning.

Her captor ignored her, black and red hair swaying in the dry breeze.

"What's your name?"

The Tainted missed a step but recovered. "Why do you want to know?"

Time for a new angle. If she couldn't get away, she'd need a friend wherever they were going. "You've bound my wounds, given me shoes, and protected me from beasts I couldn't even see," Hazel puffed. The ache in her legs lessened as they crested a saddle in the mountain. "I would like your name, so I can thank you properly."

No response.

She needed to try harder. "I'm tired of referring to you as my captor or Tainted..."

Her captor stilled and whispered, "What did you say?"

Confusion wrinkled her brow. She hadn't said

anything rude. "I said—"

Her captor stormed back to her, rage clinging to her like a cloak. Hazel leaned away as the girl bared her fangs in a hiss. She didn't relish getting bitten.

"Don't you dare use that slur!"

Slur? "I meant no offense," she rushed out. "May I ask what offended you?"

Her captor scoffed. "Like you don't know."

"I don't."

"I am not *Tainted*," the girl spat, her fangs slurring her speech. "If anyone's tainted this world by their presence, it's *you*."

She nodded and backed away, getting out of range of the sharp teeth. Those fangs were *really* scary. "My apologies. I won't use that word again." *Out loud.*

"I'd watch what you say from here on out. Others would kill for such an offense." Her captor scanned her face and her lips pulled back. "You're lucky I'm so tolerant of your heritage."

Her eyes widened when a hiccupping sound escaped her. Oh hell, she was going to laugh. She patted her chest and coughed through the hysteria. Now was not the time to laugh at the dangerous snake girl.

With a last harrumph, the vexing Tainted pulled

back and stomped away.

Hazel coughed a few more times and swallowed to wet her dry throat. That was a close one. There was no telling what the girl would do if she thought Hazel was laughing at her.

"Get moving, Chica. I won't tell you again."

The nickname was new.

She grumbled under her breath about prickly captors while she trudged up the last bit of the mountain, the scratches on her back itching all the while. A smile lifted the corners of her mouth as the strain on her thighs lessened. Boy, did it feel good to walk on flat ground. But her joy was short-lived.

"Oh, come on," she groaned, well past caring if her captor heard her. The Tainted girl was already descending the mountain. Panic tugged at her chest. This was the end for her. Once she descended, Harbor would disappear completely.

She scanned the area around her, making a mental note of the position of the sun and her surroundings. If she could leave a piece of her shirt, it would make an excellent landmark. She eyed her ripped blue tank. It had seen better days. She'd been leaving breadcrumbs the entire time in the hopes that someone would find her, or she could use it as a map to get home. *Home*. Even thinking the word hurt.

"My name is Hazel, not Chica," she said. She stole one last peek over her shoulder. *I love you. I promise I'll be back.*

"You've told me before."

Stubborn wench. Her brothers would love her captor. The thought slapped her in the face and she shook her head. The heat was getting to her. She turned her back on her only home and hiked down the hill. "What's your name?"

Silence.

They were back to that. "I won't stop asking until you answer me."

"It's Remy," the Tainted girl muttered, reaching the rocks Hazel had been eyeing.

"Remy..." she said. "That's a nice name."

"Un huh," Remy muttered. "Hurry up."

"I'm coming." An embarrassing scream burst out of her as her foot slipped and she wobbled, narrowly avoiding a huge cactus with wicked-looking spines. *Man, that would've hurt.*

Hazel edged around the evil-looking plant and picked her way down to Remy. She bent over and attempted to calm her breathing. "Can we please take a rest? I don't think I can go on much further." Her legs were practically jelly.

"Your fatigue is making you sloppy. You almost became that cactus' pincushion."

Was that a joke? She peeked at Remy, but the girl had turned her back and strode toward the giant pile of rocks. Her jaw dropped when her captor grabbed part of the rock and pulled. It wasn't rock at all, but a camouflaged entrance. She eyed the black opening. "What's that?"

"Your break."

Curious, she straightened and hobbled over to Remy's side and peeked into the inky darkness. "Where does it lead?"

"None of your business."

Remy shoved her inside, and she stumbled into the darkness, blinking repeatedly, trying to see around her. It was a small cave with some sort of vehicle inside. Remy yanked the curtain closed, cutting out the only source of light.

Darkness settled over her. Her hand snuck toward the dart, unease running up her spine. A click broke the silence, and a beam of light shone from Remy's hand, melting some of her fear. She hadn't always feared the dark, but after being in the wilds she now understood why her brothers insisted on sleeping with a lit lantern in the house.

Hazel squinted at the flashlight and snuck a glance at the vehicle. It looked similar to the side-by-sides in Harbor, except old and rusted. She could drive it. An idea formed quickly in her mind as Remy strode around the vehicle and ran her hand along one of the wheel-wells.

A triumphant smile lit her captor's face as she pulled out a key. "It's time to go."

She couldn't agree more. Her moment had finally come. That vehicle was the key to getting home unscathed.

She schooled her expression. "I'm not getting in that thing."

The Tainted took a step toward her. "Yes, you are."

"Let me go."

Remy took another step. "I can't do that. Don't make this harder than it is."

Shoulders hunched forward and head hanging, Hazel shuffled forward. All she needed was a bit of bare skin and her freedom would be in her grasp. She moved past the front end of the side-by-side.

Just a little closer.

"I hate you for this," she whispered, pausing next to Remy. "You're turning into the very thing you claim is evil."

Remy's shoulders stiffened, and she stepped into Hazel's space. *Checkmate.*

A flick of the wrist is all it took. Remy's foreign eyes widened a second before her legs folded underneath her. Hazel wrapped her arm around her captor's middle and lowered her to the ground. She avoided Remy's angry gaze as she pried the key from her hand.

"This isn't personal," she said, forcing herself to look the girl in the eye. "I'm sorry it came to this. I'm sure this is a safe place if you're willing to leave a vehicle here. I wouldn't leave you if I thought it was dangerous." Why was she explaining herself? "I have to go home. My family needs me, and…" Her jaw clenched, and she swallowed as Aaron's face flashed through her mind. "You were right. There are some dangerous, evil people in Harbor, but I will rid my home of them."

She pulled a jacket from Remy's pack and put it under her former captor's head. "Find peace, Remy." She patted the girl's head and clambered to her feet. Her heart pounded in her chest as she rounded the vehicle and painfully climbed in.

She glanced back at Remy and down to the key nestled in her fingers. "She'll survive," she whispered to herself. *She would have sold you ... or worse.*

With a shaking hand, she thrust the key into the ignition and turned it over. Nothing.

"No," she whispered and tried again. Still nothing. "Come on," she urged, trying again while pumping the gas a few times. This time, she earned a few sputters. "That's it," she crooned, petting the dashboard. "Please start for me."

Hazel revved the gas and tried again. Relief flooded her when the side-by-side coughed a few times and then started. "Thank goodness." She puffed out a breath and stroked the dash one last time for good luck. This was her ticket home. She shifted into reverse and angled it toward the opening.

A pinch.

Hazel stilled and glanced down to her arm. *Damn.* A dart.

She lifted her chin and stared across the passenger side at Remy. The girl smiled at her, all fangs.

"How?" Had she given her the wrong one? There were a couple different colors, but she'd chosen the one Remy had used on her. The room spun, and her head lulled to the side.

Fingers clenched her chin and tugged upwards, forcing her to look at one angry snake girl. Remy leaned closer and whispered, "You can't use my own venom against me. My body burns through it within seconds."

Hazel zeroed in on Remy's wicked-looking fangs and it clicked. Snake. Fangs. Venom. "I'm an idiot," she slurred as darkness claimed her.

CHAPTER TWELVE

Hazel

They say third time's the charm. Whoever *they* were, they didn't know what they were talking about. The third time being drugged sucked the most.

Sharp needles of pain stabbed behind her eyes, threatening to crack her head wide open. She pinched the bridge of her nose and moaned, "Just kill me now."

"I've put too much effort into keeping you alive."

It took a moment for the voice to register, and to remember why it filled her with fury.

Darting Remy. Almost getting away. Being drugged. Burning. Dizziness. Darkness.

She gasped at the memory and forced her eyes

open. The dark sky was in full bloom overhead, chasing the last vestiges of the sun away. How many hours had she lost to sleep? Head pounding, Hazel lifted her head to peek at her surroundings. Nothing looked familiar. Her valley was long gone. Even the terrain looked alien. She'd never seen plants or trees that were so green.

"You've been sleeping for almost two days."

Her heart picked up. *Two days.* She desperately scanned the land for anything that looked like home. Nothing. The full extent of her despair and panic seized her. Her mind whispered the insidious word she'd been avoiding. *Lost.* She was hopelessly lost.

Escape had been within her grasp and she'd failed. Carefully, she lowered her throbbing head and stared at the ripped ceiling of the ATV. Tears squeezed out of the corners of her eyes and dripped down her face. A silent sob racked her body, followed by another. It was too much. The blending, Aaron, the beasts, the Tainted men, the death march, Remy ... the tears flowed harder.

She'd always believed her mama's grit flowed through her veins, but today proved it did not. Her papa's words floated to her through a haze of pain and tears. *You're nothing like her.*

"Are you ... crying?" It was the first time Remy had sounded unsure, hesitant.

Hazel choked back a sob, hating that she couldn't even cry for what she had lost. *Never let them see you weak*, Colton had said. She closed her eyes and swallowed down her pain and a broken heart. Self-pity had no place among survival. If she wanted to survive whatever was to come, it was time to hide deep within herself and become a cold-hearted witch.

She wiped her damp cheek on her bandaged shoulder and inhaled deeply. Emotions would ruin her. If she'd been thinking with her head, not her heart, she would've knocked Remy out and left her there without a backward glance. It was a mistake, and it cost her everything.

Her home. Her family.

She blocked out her pain and sat up slowly. Her ribs cried out at their abuse, along with every other abused body part, but she ignored all of them. She felt Remy's gaze on her, but she didn't look her way. Foreign land rushed past as they bumped along in silence. Jo had told her that her compassion was the best thing about her, but that wasn't the truth. It was her innate ability to adapt to life and blend in.

Something rose in the distance, stark against the

fading sky. She stared harder. Towers jutted from the top of the bluff. An immense curved wall made of stone and metal wound around a town and connected to the bluff on either side, forming a half-moon. Crops spread out in a half-circle from the metal monstrosity that would keep her prisoner.

"What's that?" she murmured, finally glancing in Remy's direction. She already knew the answer, but she couldn't help but ask.

"Our destination."

That's what she feared. This was no ragtag group of people, but a well-operated machine. Once she entered the compound, it would swallow her up forever. "Will they kill me?"

Remy jerked, her brows furrowing. "No," A pause. "Unless you give them a reason to. Hazel..."

"Yes?"

Her captor licked her lips. "Don't give them any trouble. Things will go easier for you."

Remy was warning her? Too little, too late. "I'll keep that in mind," she replied, staring again at the compound looming ahead of them. A shiver worked through her, whether from the cold or fear, she didn't know. Grit. She had grit. This wouldn't be the end of her. She was a survivor.

Remy jerked the ATV to the side, whipping Hazel around. Her fingers dug into the seat and she glared at the back of her captor's head. "You're driving like a crazy person. I almost fell out."

"It's about to get worse."

Remy whipped the vehicle from side to side, causing her to slide back and forth in her seat. Hazel's head started spinning and she slapped a hand over her mouth. The bumps were bad enough, but with the swerving...

Her captor glanced at her in the rearview mirror and stepped on the gas. "We're being followed. Hold on tight. We can't enter the town until they're eliminated."

She grasped the seat in front of her and glanced behind her. Lobos. It was the mutant wolves. "Not them again," she moaned. "Stupid lobos."

"Wraiths."

"Wraiths?" she yelled over the wind.

"We call them wraiths, because they move like shadows and smoke. They're dangerous this time of year. Hunting in packs gives them such an advantage."

That it did. She still remembered how they appeared out of thin air beneath her tree. No sound, no warning. She locked eyes with one of the beasts and she swore it picked up speed.

"Remy," she said, trying to keep her voice steady. "They're catching up."

"I know. The avions will take care of them."

Hazel whipped around and planted herself firmly in the seat as Remy continued her mad driving. Movement on top of the wall caught her eye.

Holy. Bananas.

Giant sets of wings flared against the fading pink sunset and launched into the air. "W-w-what is that?" she stuttered. Some kind of giant bird monster?

"The avions."

Terror and awe filled her as the avions sped toward them. What would it be like to have beasts like that to protect Harbor? An aerial assault was almost unheard of these days, but it would be useful for protection. They had a few ancient drones, but they didn't do much.

A yip and motion near her side tore her eyes from the sky. It wasn't just one group of lobos. Another pack of three raced toward them from her right. "Remy..." her voice rose.

"I know."

"There's more." Closer now.

"I know!"

"Remy!" she yelled as one closed in with huge loping steps. There wasn't anywhere for her to run. If she let go of the bar above her, she'd be thrown from the vehicle.

"Ohcrapcrapcrapcrapcrap!" she yelled as it loped closer. The wraith was so close, she saw slobber dripping from its jowls. She screamed as its hind quarters bunched and it lunged for her.

Her scream cut off when something slammed into the beast from above, pinning it to the ground.

Hazel swiveled around and gasped as an avion dropped from the sky and onto the wraiths. Ice trickled into her veins as she got a good look at one. It wasn't a beast. "Tainted," she whispered.

One of the avions swiveled like he'd heard her, and their gazes locked. She felt frozen. His midnight eyes pierced her. She thought she understood terror, but it was nothing compared to the cold, empty gaze that promised death and destruction. The spell broke when he turned from her and launched into the air, his stark wings blending into the sky.

"Oh, God," she whispered, watching the surrounding destruction. Her gaze skipped back to the chain-link fence that had slid open. Remy slowed, and all she could focus on was that she'd be caged with these monsters. Would they tear her open like they did to the wraiths? What had Remy led her to?

She gauged the speed and Remy's attention. If she planned it right, she could run for the trees. It was dark enough that no one would see her. She blew out a breath and steadied herself, counting her heartbeats while watching Remy out of the corner of her eye. Her captor was waving at someone near the first fence. It was now or never.

Hazel slid from the ATV and stumbled, crashing to one knee, her right hand steadying her. Pain ran up and down her legs, but she could handle it. She pushed herself to her feet and crouched low, running as fast as possible without attracting attention. Her skin pebbled as she waited for the alarm. Once someone noticed she was gone, she had to give it her all. *One, two, three, four, five...*

A shout, and commotion.

That's all she needed. Straightening, she burst into a sprint. Her feet pounded against the earth in rhythm with her breathing. Her lungs and legs burned, but she didn't slow. If she made it to the tree line, she'd make it. The forest was dense enough to provide cover from the monsters in the air. Her legs trembled, but they held steady.

Thirty feet, twenty feet, ten…

Whooshing filled her ears; an arm wrapped around her waist, halting her. Hazel screamed and kicked her feet out to throw her attacker's balance off. It did nothing except knock the wind out of her.

"Going somewhere?" a deep, dangerous voice drawled.

"Let me go, you bastard!" She raked her fingernails along the muscular arm wrapped below her chest.

"Wrong answer, blondie."

She sucked in one breath, then blinding agony seared along her nerves and the ground fell away. If she could have screamed, it would have been a blessing. His arms had wrapped around her broken one, pinning it to her body. The pain and terror built and built until Hazel didn't exist anymore, only the ravenous pain ravaging her body.

Make it stop. For the love of all that's holy. Make. It. Stop.

Her nails dug into the bands of steel wrapped around her waist in an attempt to ground herself, but it did nothing. The world tilted and blurred, but the pain kept on burning. When her feet finally touched the ground, she hardly noticed. Her body collapsed on itself and she trembled against the ground. Blurred shapes moved around her like a live watercolor painting.

A dark blur leaned in, its clawed hands reaching for her. A whimper passed her cracked lips, and she wanted to move away, to run, but her body wouldn't cooperate. She wasn't in control of it. *Never in control...*

Terror caused her to tremble harder as the claws brushed her hair from her face. It didn't hurt. The fingers were gentle, soft as they offered her comfort.

"Hazel?" The voice was familiar, but her lips wouldn't form the words to reply. *Remy.*

Someone whistled. "You found an Untouched?"

"I think that's apparent," Remy snarled. "It's okay, Hazel. Everything will be okay."

Nothing was okay. She had a demon inside her, hell bent on burning her alive.

"She's in shock," a man said.

"Aren't you the brilliant one?" Remy snarked. "Of *course* she's in shock, Jameson! Our fearless leader caused it."

"She fled. She couldn't be allowed to escape," said a deep voice. "She was already bleeding. I didn't cause that."

It sent skitters of fear, and something else she

171

couldn't name, down Hazel's spine. It was the kind of voice that, in the deep of night, sent longing or terror through you. Danger and sin.

All thoughts of danger and sin fled her mind when clawed fingertips brushed her broken arm. Hazel jerked and cried out. Couldn't they tell the pain was eating her from the inside? That each touch was a torture of its own?

An inky shadow knelt near her broken arm. Something wild and spicy teased her nose.

"I didn't know her arm was broken." A growled curse. "I need to reset it."

"Nooooooo," she moaned, eyelids squeezing shut. *No more pain.*

Searing agony shot up her arm, causing her back to arch. Would her suffering ever end?

"Shhhhh…" Remy crooned, humming a little song. It was achingly familiar. One her mama used to sing. "She needs medical attention."

"And you think she deserves it?" the dark voice asked.

Silence.

"She deserves a chance … and she's way too valuable to lose to injuries and infection."

Hazel wanted to scoff. Once the fire stopped

burning inside her, there would be nothing left to heal. Someone scooped her up, angering the vengeful beast inside of her, and nestled her against a broad, warm chest. She sighed and cuddled closer to the warmth and let herself fall into the gentle swaying. The arms around her stiffened and the gentle sway stopped. Why did it stop? *Please don't stop.*

A heavy sniff, and the body holding hers stiffened completely.

"Are you serious?" Remy demanded.

The swaying began again, pulling a sigh from her. It was exquisite torture to be held in such a sweet way while in agony. Sweet agony. She never knew the meaning until now.

"Noah?"

"It doesn't matter." His voice vibrated her cheek, holding an edge.

"If you think so, then you're in for a world of hurt," Remy said softly.

"You've got to be kidding me," another male burst out. "How long have you been waiting?"

"Not another word, Jameson." The arms shifted her. "Let Doc know that we have a new patient."

"Where do you want him to meet us?" the other male asked.

"The prison."

Voices rose around her. Prison? She hoped it had a roof. There were monsters outside. Flying monsters. Her fingers clenched the shirt underneath her cheek.

"Please," she croaked. "Please don't let the monsters get me."

The voices quieted.

She tightened her grip. "Please," she begged.

"I won't," he said hesitantly.

"Thank you," she whispered.

A prick.

She knew that feeling well. Maybe the fourth time was a charm.

CHAPTER THIRTEEN

Hazel

Hazel blinked her eyes open, staring at the red stone ceiling above her. For a moment, her life was normal, her mind wiped free of memory.

Someone shifted, and she turned her head, confused. Then, she saw the monster lounging against the wall across from the foot of her bed.

She screamed.

There was nothing—*nothing*—more monstrous than the obsidian eyes pinning her to her spot. A shudder worked through her as she eyed the black scales dusting his high cheekbones and strong jaw line. It was only when his black leather wings rising above his shoulders flared slightly that Hazel jerked back. It took her a second to process that her good arm was cuffed to the bed—*the monsters had cuffed her to the bed*. Blinding terror moved through her veins, causing her to shake.

Outrunning the wraiths. Flying monsters. Being captured. Agony. Voices. Drugs.

She gasped at the memory, her ragged breathing the only sound in the room. It seemed impossible that she was alive. She had been sure there'd be nothing left of her once the demon inside had burned everything to ash.

"I survived," she whispered through trembling, cracked lips.

"So it seems," the dark monster replied from where he reclined against the wall, looking for all the world like a predator—sleek, deadly, powerful.

She glanced around the room for something, anything to defend herself with. There was nothing. It was a glorified cave with smooth curving walls, presumably in the fortress she had seen in the distance.

Her hand clenched around the chain cuffing her to the old medical bed, and she yanked. She had to get out. It didn't budge. Her gaze flickered to the monster still watching her, then back to the chain. Another yank. Her hand slipped, and pain bloomed around her wrist.

If they didn't let her die, then what did they plan on doing to her? Dread filled her belly.

"Do you really think you can get away?"

Hazel yelped and scooted back as far as the chain would let her. Despite the hard gleam in his eyes, his wicked lips curved in a cruel smile, one that said he was laughing at her, enjoying her fear. Cool air caressed her collarbone, causing her to freeze. She glanced down at herself. Her shirt and bra were gone. Her legs tensed, the homespun sheets teasing her skin.

Naked. Someone had stripped her and seen her naked. Her eyes slid to the silent monster assessing her with a frown. What did he want with her? What had Remy led her to? Her death, or something much worse?

Noticing her attention, he arched a brow and crossed his scaled forearms across his broad chest.

Hazel dropped her eyes to her heaving chest and stared. Her arm had been bandaged and put into a proper sling. She wiggled her toes and felt cloth digging into the skin of her arches.

Had the monster tended to her? Her blood beneath her skin began to burn with horror and embarrassment. What else had he done?

She sucked in a shaky inhale and forced herself to meet the eyes of her silent captor. She opened her mouth and hesitated. *Grit, Hazel. Dig deep for your grit.*

"Who did this?" The words lingered in the air. He cocked his head, shiny black hair sliding over his proud brow. Her skin prickled as he just stared. She almost expected him not to answer.

"Doc." One word. Lovely.

"Pass along my thanks," she said. A kind word went a long way to paving the road for civility. And boy, did she need civility.

"It wasn't done for your benefit."

His words cut like a whip. Hazel forced herself not to cower at the way he threw the vehement words at her. Predators liked it when their prey cowered or ran. She needed to show herself not to be prey.

"Let me go." Her words were soft but strong. Her voice never wavered.

"You're going to make demands of me?" The words were barely a whisper but held an edge of steel.

"I've done nothing wrong. You have no reason to hold me."

"You're no innocent," he scoffed. "I have every reason to hold you."

"I've done nothing to your people. I wish to go home," she pleaded. "Please let me go home."

Anger seemed to gather around him like a storm. He stepped closer, causing her heart to pound in her chest. "Step any closer and I'll scream," she said. There had to be someone nearby who would help her or step in.

His smile exposed two slightly long canines, but they had nothing on Remy's fangs. "You think they'll help you?" His voice slithered along her nerves, ratcheting up her terror. "You are very far from home, Untouched." She cringed away as he moved around the bed, his midnight wing grazing her leg. Everything inside her stilled and her eyes widened when he leaned over her. "No one will help a killer."

Up close he was even more terrifying. She wasn't sure if she should look him in his fathomless eyes or stare at the scales on his cheeks. "I've never killed anyone," she mumbled through numb lips, terror making it hard to form words.

His lips curled back over his teeth as he eyed her.

"Why are you here?"

"Because you forced me to be," she whispered.

He held up a finger, tipped with a short, pointed black nail. "That is lie number one. Your time is short. I suggest you choose your words wisely, or they may be your last."

A spark of anger caught in her gut. She'd told the truth from the beginning. It wasn't her fault she was here. "I am telling the truth," she forced out through clenched teeth.

He lifted his hand toward her face, and she jolted. A smirk curled the corners of his mouth as she strained against the chains and turned her face away. Her pulse went into overdrive as a sharp claw traced her jaw.

"You're so plain. No wonder you came out of the wilds unscathed. You'd hardly be worth anything at the market."

Market? Like hell. Hazel turned toward him and spit right in his face. She blinked, and horror washed over her as her saliva dipped down his face.

He lifted an arm and wiped his face before meeting her gaze with a savage grin. "There's the hatred I was looking for. It's easy to spot if you know which buttons to push."

"You're disgusting."

"Backatcha, blondie." He placed his hands on the bed near her hips and stared her down. "Who sent you?"

"No one sent me."

"That's lie number two," he said.

"I'm not lying," she stuttered.

"I wonder if they pick you just for your innocent look. No one would guess you a viper."

A hysterical laugh slipped from her. This monster was as crazy as Remy. "No one is a viper here, except the one you use to kidnap innocent people like myself."

A deep chuckle rumbled from his chest. Hazel scowled as goosebumps erupted on her arms. He leaned into her space again, his nose almost touching hers.

"You're good. No wonder Remy is all out of sorts," he said, his words whispering across her skin. "I wonder how you would hold up under ... other interrogation methods." His claws skittered across her sheet—the only thing covering her.

Other interrogation methods ... understanding dawned. Hazel's finger's curled into the sheet. "I'd die first before I'd let you touch me, you tainted monster."

Something flashed through his gaze, but it was gone before she could decipher its meaning. He gave her a satisfied smile and stepped away, the air cooling around her immediately. She gaped at his wings as he strode toward the door, the tips almost touching the floor. He pounded his fist against the metal door three times quickly.

"Remember, I gave you a chance," he said.

That was a joke. She was a logical person and knew what he was up to. "No, you didn't. You ignored everything I said, and that's on you," she called as the door opened. "Stop pretending you're trying to help me. We both know you wish me to burn."

He glanced over his shoulder, his face unreadable. "You can't fool me with pretty words."

"I'm sure, but you're blinded by your own hate and cast it on me," she said steadily, her heart galloping in her chest. "I wish to speak to your leader."

"You're a prisoner. You get no requests."

Her stomach quivered as she steeled herself for her next words. "I do if you want any information out of me whatsoever. I'm sure your leader would hate to hear of your unwillingness to grant me this one thing in exchange for something you seek." It was a gamble. She didn't have any information that he wanted to hear.

He eyed her in disgust. "I am the leader, and I don't negotiate with mass murderers."

With that parting remark, he disappeared and slammed the door. The sound echoed in the room and reverberated in her mind.

Mass murderer? Who did he think she was?

CHAPTER FOURTEEN

Hazel

She didn't sleep.

Every sound made her jump and her pulse leap, but the worst was the absolute darkness. No matter how hard she strained, she couldn't see a damn thing. She almost cried when a man with auburn hair carrying a tray and a lantern arrived.

She blinked back the tears and watched silently as he placed the lantern down on an old wooden table. Next, the tray full of medical supplies. He was normal, and he'd brought soup. *Savory soup.* Her mouth watered, and her cheeks warmed when her stomach growled.

He smiled and leaned against the table, crossing his ankles. "How are you feeling?"

There wasn't disdain or malice in his tone, just a question. Something loosened inside her chest. "Fine," she whispered.

"You can do better than that."

Her gaze darted to the open doorway, where a bulky shadow stood just out of the light. Fear kept her mouth shut. There was no telling what they were reporting back to their fearsome leader.

The man's red brows slashed together as he glanced in the direction she was staring. "Close the door, Jameson."

"You sure, Doc? That goes against my instructions."

Doc scowled. "I don't care what he bloody well says. The girl deserves some privacy. Close the door."

"Fine, but it's your butt when he hears of this," Jameson grumbled, closing the door.

Her breath came a little more easily with the door closed. She shifted her gaze to Doc and stifled a gasp. Not normal. His tangle of red hair had hidden his true form. Pointed red and white ears popped up and swiveled toward her. *Tainted. Another monster.* How stupid was she? She was in a Tainted compound. Why would she assume there was anyone human here?

She cringed against her pillow, wishing the bed would swallow her when he stepped closer with a bowl of something that smelled herby. "What is that?" she barked. Was it another drug? If he tried to force anything on her, she'd bite him. They might have tied her down, but at least they hadn't gagged her. Putrid breath and a bandana flashed through her mind.

He scanned her face and slowly set the bowl back onto the table. "It's something for the pain and infection."

"I don't want it." She never wanted to be drugged again.

Doc studied her. "I'm not going to hurt you."

The pain after her escape rushed back to her. The monsters didn't care for her wellbeing. She shook her head to dispel the memory. "I don't believe you. What do you want?" He was here for something. She'd seen and heard the disdain the monsters had for her. There was no way he was here *just* to help.

"To help you heal."

"For what purpose?" There was always a purpose.

"What other reason would there be but for you to heal?" he asked, lips pursed.

He was playing a game with her. "You tell me."

"So suspicious." He tsked. "I'm not here to harm you."

"Any worse than you already have, you mean?"

His ears laid back. "Your injuries are not my doing."

"But they are your leader's."

The holes in her memory had slowly filtered back in last night. Her agony had been caused by *him*. Her stomach clenched every time she thought back to flying. She'd never felt so helpless in her life.

"He didn't know," Doc said, picking up the bowl and moving toward her again.

She scooted as far away from him as possible, but he kept coming. Hazel yelped when he lifted the sheet, exposing her stomach. He averted his gaze, made sure her important bits were covered, then dipped his fingers into the green paste and gently smoothed it across the myriad of bruises and cuts.

"You're a mess," he commented. "You're lucky you survived your injuries."

Luck had nothing to do with it. Maybe bad luck. She glanced away and stared at the wall. "It would've been better if I died."

His cool fingers paused. "Has someone hurt you?"

The answer was obvious, but she understood what he alluded to. She didn't want to answer, but the fear of him doing an examination had her spewing the venomous words she'd locked inside. "Not for lack of trying." The words tasted like ash on her tongue. She could almost feel her cheek throbbing in memory of Aaron backhanding her.

"I'm sorry," he whispered as he slowly draped the sheet over her belly and moved to her bandaged feet. Hazel refused to meet his russet eyes and zoned out as he went about his business. Only when he held a spoon out to her did she respond.

"No." She stared him down, lips firmly pressed together.

His rust-colored eyes narrowed on her. "You have to eat."

Her stomach growled, punctuating his words. She ignored her belly and glared at his hand. "I said no."

She'd stayed up all night analyzing her conversation with the Tainted from the day before. Everything he'd said led her to the conclusion they were keeping her alive to extend her torture, to sell her to the highest bidder, or turn her into some sort of amusement. None of those options were acceptable. She'd beat them at their own game.

"Not eating will solve nothing."

She kept her mouth shut. Doc huffed out a breath and lowered the soup. He placed it carefully near her cuffed hand. "If you change your mind, it's right here."

She watched as he cleaned up his supplies and left

the room without another glance. The smell of the savory soup caused her stomach to cramp painfully. Hazel slapped the wooden bowl off the bed and silently mourned as the delicious-smelling soup splattered all over the dusty floor.

It was done. She couldn't go back now.

"You have to eat! So help me, I'll force it down your throat if I have to," Doc growled.

Hazel stared back at him, her face a blank mask. No one would ever make her do something she didn't want to again. He'd visited her twice a day for the last week, along with others. Various terrifying Tainted had observed her and tried their hand for information. They all seemed to think she was some sort of spy for a homicidal group of people. Her people.

She'd tried to tell them the truth. The people of Harbor were peaceful. She'd never hurt anyone. No one listened, so she stopped speaking. They obviously wanted her to confess to something she didn't do. Honestly, she was tempted a few times, but she wouldn't give them the satisfaction. It was one thing for her to take the blame, and another to give her enemies a reason to strike at Harbor. Her blank persona worked well for her. She'd been gathering information on the Tainted that had visited her and she'd come to an alarming realization. Harbor was vastly out-manned. The Tainted had abilities that her people could never compete with.

"Are you listening to me?" Doc threw his hand in the air in an uncharacteristic show of anger. She'd learned a bit about the Tainted doctor in the last week. He was professional, gentle, and had a dry sense of humor. She almost liked him.

He stabbed a finger at her. "This cannot continue. I refuse to watch you kill yourself. I've already set you up with an IV, so you can't die of dehydration. Don't force my hand, Hazel."

She jolted at her name.

He dipped his chin to meet her eyes. "That's right, Hazel. I know your name. No thanks to you, I might add."

Hazel blinked at him and turned her face away to stare at the rough wall.

"So be it."

She didn't turn when he slammed the door shut or when he began yelling outside of her cell. It didn't matter. None of it mattered. Her eyes closed, and she drifted in her thoughts and memories. Happy ones.

Hours passed, and Doc didn't come back for his second visit. The dull light from the bars in her door faded into nothing and darkness descended. She still hadn't gotten used to the total darkness. She had to keep her eyes closed, so as not to panic. It was stifling, and too quiet.

No matter how many times she tried to sleep, she couldn't. Tears gathered behind her lids and silently slipped out, each an admission of misery and weakness. She missed her family, her mama, and Matt. She choked back a sob. No matter how many stories she'd read, there was no such thing as happily ever after. Life was cruel, and then you died.

She sniffled and lifted her hand to wipe the corner of her eye, her cuff sliding across the metal bar of her bed. She paused and twisted her wrist. The cuff was looser. She pulled, and her hand slid out a little before catching. Disbelief and hope warred in her chest. Could she get out?

She slowly sat up, her ribs smarting, and pulled harder. The metal bit into the fleshy part of her hand. Hazel wiggled her hand back and forth. No give, only discomfort. Sweat beaded on her brow and she bit her lip, pulling harder. Wicked hell, it hurt. If only she had something wet to grease the metal.

Her eyes flickered behind her lids and she frantically looked for options. The saline solution wouldn't help. The healing paste Doc had used on her had already dried on her skin so that was out. Spit? No, that wouldn't work either. She tugged again at her wrist and pain flared.

Blood. The thought came unbidden to her. She inhaled deeply and clenched her jaw. What was a little pain when it came to freedom?

Nothing worth doing was ever easy. Her papa always said that.

Seconds turned to minutes, and minutes into hours. It turned out that it was a lot harder to cut yourself with a blunt cuff than she imagined. When she finally did manage to do it, the pain was so bad she blacked out. Or at least, she thought she did. One couldn't tell when it was pitch dark.

Liquid dripped down her arm and pooled in her elbow. Soon, it dried and became sticky. Over and over, she aggravated her wound to slicken her cuff. Dull light began to filter back into her room, and she stared at the mess she'd made. The once tan sheet was now a grisly painting, her wrist a mangled mess that made her want to puke.

She breathed through it and began her efforts anew. She glanced at the door occasionally, her panic doubling. Doc would be here soon, and with him, her escape would disappear. She yanked harder, biting back her yelp of pain. Voices filtered in through the barred window in her door. Her time was up.

Hazel yanked viciously, a whimper of pain escaping her closed lips. The cuff scraped over her knuckles. She lifted her free hand and stared in awe. *I did it.* Her joy was short-lived, though. Her door swung open and Doc stormed in. He skidded to a stop, his eyes rounding.

She pulled her wounded wrist to her chest. Warmth seeped through the sheet and onto her chest. They stared at each other for a moment before Doc held his hands up slowly as if to soothe her.

"Hazel, honey, are you okay?" he asked softly.

"I'm fine." She was. It was just a little blood. Well, a lot of blood. "It looks worse than it is."

"Doc, I smell blood."

She jerked at the male voice outside of the door. *The monster.*

Her eyes connected with Doc's for one second before she threw herself out of the bed, tearing the sheet from it as she moved. The IV in her arm burned as she tilted the IV rod in front of her.

Black wings were the first things she noticed as the monster burst into the room. She kept her eyes on him. He and Doc were both monsters, but the scaled one was the most dangerous one in the room.

His midnight gaze swept the room and he inhaled deeply, his nostrils flaring as his eyes settled on her. Her legs quivered beneath her and the room spun. Days without food had not helped her. "Stay back," she yelled.

"We're not going to hurt you," Doc said, stepping closer.

"Lies," she hissed. If she didn't kill herself, they would. This was her choice. She was in control.

Doc took another step closer. "Honey, put down your IV. I need to look at your wrist. You're bleeding all over the place."

She bared her teeth at the monster who stood like a statue. "No. You'll never take me alive."

"Hazel, please let me help you. I'll send him away."

The sheet slipped a little to reveal the top of one breast, but she didn't care. The whole world could see her naked if it meant she could escape. "You want to help me?"

"You know I do."

"Then let me go."

Silence.

"I can't do that, honey."

A bitter smile twisted her lips. "You say can't…" She met Doc's eyes. "I say won't."

It only took one moment for her escape attempt to end. She knew she shouldn't have taken her eyes off the predator in the room. The monster launched over her bed and moved toward her. She swiped at him with her IV, but it did nothing. The monster plucked it from her hand and yanked her off her feet. For one moment, she was airborne, and the next, she was pinned to the bed.

Her breath came in heavy pants. She bucked and screamed, but it did nothing. Flashes of Aaron and the pig man swirled in her mind. "Nononononono," she cried. "Get off me!" Tears blurred her eyes, distorting the monster leaning over her.

"Noah, you're making it worse."

The monster on top of her yelled, "She's hurting herself, Doc." A choking sound. "There's so much blood."

"She's not badly hurt."

"There's blood everywhere!" he snarled.

The sound made the hair on her arms rise. Primal.

Dangerous. Deadly. Her body shook harder. Something soft brushed her cheek. Hazel turned her face into the warmth and shuddered out a breath. She opened her eyes and bile burned the back of her throat.

A wing. It was the monster's bloody wing.

She jerked away and caught the onyx-eyed brute staring down at her with something akin to wonder. Her stomach rolled. "Get off me! I'm going to puke."

His gaze shuttered, and he shifted to the side as she leaned over the bed to heave. Bile flooded her mouth, but nothing else came up. Tears, blood, and bile mixed on the floor. A hand smoothed down her hair and a voice crooned, "That's it, honey. It's okay. Doc's going to take care of you. No one will hurt you."

She pulled back, collapsing on the bed. Her wrist pulsed with her heartbeat. With every second that passed, her eyelids drooped. Voices rose around her, but she didn't care. All she wanted was a nap. Maybe she would go to sleep and never wake up. A pinch to the inside of her elbow had her eyes springing open.

Doc stared down at her with worried eyes. "Hazel! Can you hear me?"

"Leave me alone," she moaned. Why couldn't everyone leave her alone?

"Now's not the time," the monster stated.

"So help me, Noah," said another voice, "if you don't let me in that room, I will go right through you. You and Remy have both kept her from me long enough. Get out of my way."

Hazel frowned. She knew that voice. Where did she know that voice from?

Doc glared over her shoulder at someone. "You two pipe down," he snarled. "I need to stop the bleeding. Either help or get the hell out."

A cool hand brushed her forehead and along her cheek. "Baby, I need you to look at me."

She knew that voice. From where?

So tired. Her eyes closed. Lips pressed against her eyelids.

"Get your lips off of her."

"Go pound sand, Noah."

Something about that voice...

"Baby, please, please open your eyes for me. *Please.*"

Something in his voice called to her. His pleading about broke her heart.

Hazel forced her eyes open. She squinted as the room spun and the person before her solidified. She blinked and whispered, "Matt." He was alive. *Alive.*

Jerking her hand from Doc's, she placed a bloody hand against Matt's cheek. Tears slipped from her eyes. He was *here*. With her. *Alive*. "You're alive."

"I'm here. I'll always be here." He pressed his cheek into her palm and smiled at her.

Her happiness fizzled out, horror taking its place.

Fangs. He had fangs.

CHAPTER FIFTEEN

Hazel

"Please look at me."

Hazel kept her face averted, cocked her head, and squinted at where the ceiling rounded into the rough stone wall. It drove her nuts that there weren't any corners. A weird, random thought, but she'd been thinking lots of random things in the last three days to help her ignore the specter who wouldn't give her a moment's peace.

Out of the corner of her eye, she peeked at the monster version of her long-lost friend. She hated everything about him. He'd been at her side since she'd woken up three days ago. She had never been prone to passing out, but her body had been through a lot in the last several weeks and could only handle so much.

He reached for her, and she scooted away from him, his fingertips just barely grazing her arm. The monster who wore Matt's face scowled; his fingers curled into a fist, which he dropped limply into his lap. She longed to reach out and erase the sorrow and anger from his face. It was killing her not to speak to him. But she had to remember he wasn't *her* Matt. This Matt was a trickster. A liar. A deserter.

This Matt had broken her heart.

"Hazel, you need to eat something."

She gazed dispassionately at the little square window high above to her left, a small shaft of light pouring through. Dust motes danced in the light in a jolly way she wished she could capture. All she felt these days was fatigue, pain, and rage that she kept banked. Matt began to speak, and she tuned him out, imagining a dull buzzing instead of his soft, hypnotic voice.

The sun seemed to taunt her from the window. What she wouldn't give to go outside and feel the cool breeze on her face. She grunted. What a joke. She was kidding herself. The breeze was never cold. It was always hot and dry, but it was a lovely daydream anyway.

She sighed and played with the loose edge of the gauze that hung from her wrist. The cuffs had disappeared the day she tried to escape.

The day you almost killed yourself.

Hazel shut that train of thought down and ignored the shame that threatened to drown her. If she didn't eat soon, she would die. The thought didn't frighten her as much as it should have. What really bothered her was that she never had a moment alone. She had a jailor watching her every moment of each day. Nights were the worst. She'd barely gotten a wink of sleep. It was bad enough having someone watch her at night, but add the pitch black darkness to the mix and it was utterly terrifying.

"Baby, you can't go on like this."

She jerked and glared at his hand that had brushed her forearm. His chair groaned as he sat back, and she met his gaze for the first time in two days. She couldn't help the flinch. His slitted pupils made her skin crawl. It was disorienting. He still looked like Matt, except for the eyes — her gaze dropped to his mouth — and the fangs he'd been hiding.

It felt like someone stabbed her every time she looked at him. It was too much. She'd mourned him, cried herself to sleep too many nights to count, tears staining her pillow. Seeing his face worn by a monster was cruelty at its best. Her Matt wouldn't have hurt her like this. Her Matt would've come back for her. This wasn't her Matt.

"Baby…" he began.

She sliced a hand through the air. "Don't call me that. I'm not your baby. I'm not your anything."

His reptilian eyes narrowed, and Hazel shuddered.

"Do not make me force that soup down your throat again. It wasn't fun the first time."

His demanding tone was like sandstone against her skin. An ember of anger flared in her gut at the memory of Doc and Matt force-feeding her. It was a messy, tiring affair that she didn't want to repeat, but she would if they ganged up on her again. "You wouldn't dare."

"Try me," he growled.

The stubborn expression on his face was too much; she had to glance away. It was easy to pretend she didn't care about him when she wasn't looking at his stupid face, but the black hollows beneath his eyes tugged at her heart. She didn't want to care about this Matt; she wanted to hate him, but it seemed impossible. The best she could come up with was feigning apathy.

"Do what you want with me," she said, licking her

cracked lips. "I don't care. Nothing matters." Or at least that was the lie she was telling herself.

"My Hazel would've never said something like that. She wouldn't let herself waste away to nothing for no reason. The girl I knew didn't want to die. She loved to laugh, snuck peapods from the farm when no one was looking, and hoarded dried flowers like they were going out of style. That girl was full of life." He waved a hand at her. "She wasn't this poor reflection."

All those things were true, but they felt completely foreign now. When Aaron had pushed her from the Jeep, he'd destroyed part of her. Hazel tipped her head back to stare at the ceiling, mourning the girl she used to be. "Part of that girl died when my Matt did," she whispered. It was partly the truth. She'd lost some of her naïvety when he'd died, but she'd truly lost part of herself when she'd left Harbor.

"I came back for you."

She twisted around to stare at him. "Don't you dare lie to me. If you had come back for me, I wouldn't be here."

He gave her a pleading look. "There is so much you don't know that I need to explain to you, if only you'd listen to what's happened since I've last saw you."

Hazel shook her head. "I don't want to hear anything you have to say. Please be quiet, so I can go to sleep." She closed her eyes and leaned her head back on the pillow, ignoring the heavy statement.

Matt heaved a sigh. "You're obviously not ready to hear what I have to say, but when you are, I'll still be here. You can't drive me away. It won't happen."

He pushed from his chair, and she forced herself to hold still and keep her eyes closed as he pulled the blanket up to her chin. His gaze on her was like a physical thing.

"I won't let you die," he murmured. "I won't let that happen, and neither will Doc or Noah."

Noah. A shiver worked down her spine at the name. He was the worst of the Tainted. A true monster. "I'm not stupid."

"What was that?"

Hazel's eyes popped open and she stared at Matt, hiding her fear, forcing scorn into her voice. "I'm worth too much to let die. I'll fetch a much higher price at auction if I'm healthy."

He sucked in a breath, his face blanketed in shock. "We're not going to sell you."

She laughed and rolled over onto her side, giving him her back. Pain radiated from her ribs, but the pain was easier to ignore than the emotional torture she experienced when looking at her former friend. "Go away."

"If it's not me, it'll be someone else. Doc's busy helping other people, so you know who that leaves."

"I'm not afraid." *Not very much.*

"I can smell it all over you."

A lump formed in her throat, preventing her from asking the question. *Could he literally smell the fear on her?* "Leave me alone."

A frustrated growl rumbled behind her, followed by slow, booted footsteps. The door squeaked as Matt pulled it open on rusty hinges. "Despite what you believe, I'm not the monster you think I am."

"Lies," she whispered.

Her shoulders hunched up as a loud curse exploded out of him.

"Always so stubborn."

He slammed the door, and the sound reverberated through her. Tears slipped out of the corners of her eyes. No matter how much he protested it, Matt was a monster. He shouldn't have been able to hear her, and yet he could.

But even knowing that, she wanted to call out, to beg him not to leave her alone in this desolate, empty place. "I miss you," she whispered to the empty room.

How much more torture could she take before she broke?

Awareness slowly filtered in, and colors danced behind her lids. Her eyes shifted as each pain and ache made itself known. Hazel yanked and snuggled in the blanket, clinging onto sleep for a few moments more.

A painful gasp exploded from her as she bolted upright, her pulse thundering in her ears. Hazel jerked her blond hair from her face, not taking her gaze from the monster perched next to her bed. Well, perched wasn't exactly the right word. He lounged in the simple wooden chair like he was holding court in his kingdom.

She attempted to hide her unease and fear by adjusting the blanket wrapped around her. Her motions stilled as his wings twitched. She gazed at them in horrified fascination. Other than his wings, he didn't move or make a sound. It didn't even look like he was breathing.

Disturbed, she shifted on the bed and scooted a little farther away from him. His dark gaze tracked her movements, but she didn't care. She needed more space between them. Not that it would do any good. He moved like a predator, silently, swiftly.

The silence continued for many minutes until Hazel couldn't take the staring game anymore. His dark eyes seemed to pierce her stole and see right through her.

"What do you want?" she growled, wrapping her fear and anger around her like a cloak.

He cocked his head and kept quiet. It was eerie how he did that. Inhuman. She rubbed the goosebumps on her arms. He wasn't human. Why would she expect him to act in a human way? Every time he visited, it unraveled her, and she hated it. Doc she could handle and Matt she could ignore, but the winged monster … Noah – not that she'd ever use his name, he didn't deserve a name, not when he was so dangerous and scary – his scales and wings were hard to ignore.

She almost jumped out of her skin when he broke the silence. "I'm wondering when you'll be done with your tantrum," he said, his voice low like two rocks rubbed together.

"A tantrum? You haven't seen me throw a tantrum."

"From where I'm sitting, you've been throwing a tantrum since you got here. You've treated your friend like rubbish. You've been disrespectful to Doc and spat in the face of our hospitality. You're acting like a spoiled brat."

Hazel glared at him, her eyes narrowing. *How dare he!*

"I'm acting like a spoiled brat? Excuse me for not thanking you for my incarceration."

He snorted. "If I trusted you enough not to terrorize everyone around you and cause destruction, I'd let you out of this place."

It was her turn to snort. "Lies."

"If you thought about anything but your own worries, you'd see that you've been given food, a bed, shelter, clothing, and a healer for your injuries." His wings shifted behind his back as if agitated. "A doctor, I might add, that has many more patients and concerns than just you. Not to mention how abominably you've treated Matt, a man who's your friend," he said, scorn in every word.

Hazel bristled, some of her fear evaporating at his attack. "Please forgive me for not thanking my jailors for their hospitality," she hissed. "And Matt is *not* my friend." Those words weren't exactly true, but she wouldn't take them back, even though her stomach dropped when the monster's face darkened and he seemed to swell in his seat.

"Despite what Matt says about you, I don't believe him. You are still as prejudiced and monstrous as I thought in the beginning."

"Says the man who chained the girl up and threatened her with rape." The words seemed to burn her mouth as she spat them at him. How dare he pretend to be the righteous one in the situation!

He pressed his lips together, and she could've sworn a look of shame crossed his face, but it was gone as quickly as it came, replaced by his rock impression.

"I would've never done that."

"In my experience, talk is cheap, and men go to great lengths to get what they want." She swallowed against the shame of what Aaron and the pig man had done.

He studied her, his dark eyes giving nothing away. "That's not far from the truth." He sighed and then ran a hand through his hair, releasing her from his magnetic gaze and staring at the far wall absently. "Doc tells me that it would be good for you to get out into the light."

Hazel squashed the little kernel of hope that unfurled in her chest and shoved it down ruthlessly. This was probably another ploy. Was it a bribe? What did they want from her? She immediately averted her attention to the far wall when she noticed the monster was observing her. Hopefully, she had hidden how much she longed to be outside.

"You're not strong enough yet to leave. If you get yourself healthy, we can talk about taking you outside for a walk."

A walk. Like she was a dog. An animal they could

do what they wanted with. Something to be leashed. Disgust rolled through her. Lost to her thoughts, she jumped when he stood abruptly from his chair, his form blotting out the lantern light with his huge wings.

He didn't step any closer, but it still felt like he was too close. He was enormous and intimidating. The lantern light caught on the onyx scales that ran up his arms and across his cheekbones. So alien, so foreign, and yet ... there was a bitty part of her that found him appealing, interesting even. The beauty of his leathery wings and scales seemed unfair. A creature of darkness didn't deserve beauty. It deserved to look like a gargoyle.

Hazel brushed aside her errant thoughts and pretended they didn't exist.

His lip curled in loathing. "I personally don't care if you live or die. If you die, it's one less mouth I have to feed. One less person I have to care for. One less person I have to keep safe against all the things in this world that are trying to kill us. The decision is up to you. I won't force you to eat like Doc and Matt will. Live or die, it's your choice. Just stop playing with the emotions of my people."

Her eyes snagged on the small but sharp blade he produced from one of his pockets. He placed it on the end of the bed.

"This is yours. Do with it what you will."

Hazel glared at him accusingly. "Is this a joke?" she asked flatly. Why in the world would he give her a blade? Surely, he didn't think her stupid enough to take it.

A shrug. "Doc mentioned you don't like being vulnerable."

What sort of game was he playing? "So, you're handing me a weapon? Your enemy?"

"You've made the decision to be my enemy."

She didn't reach for it. She wanted to. Boy, how she wanted to. But she didn't want to be made a fool when he snatched it back. Another thought entered her mind. "Do you want me to kill myself?"

He stilled. "I want you to make a decision."

And with that, the monster left her room.

CHAPTER SIXTEEN

Noah

He inhaled deeply and forced his feet away from her door, all the while listening to what went on in the room. He turned the corner and came face-to-face with both Doc and Matt. Each man lounged against a hallway wall, their gazes focused on him.

They stayed silent as they all listened to what the girl did.

The sheets rustled, and Noah held his breath. Doc had railed against this plan. He didn't want Hazel to have access to anything she could hurt herself with. But Matt believed she wouldn't hurt herself, and Noah believed the same. Not for the same reasons as the other man, but he kept his own reasons to himself.

He did release a soft breath as he heard her put the blade underneath her pillow. He knew she wouldn't hurt herself. She had too much fight, too much of a will to live. No matter what she said, she still cared for Matt, but hurt was riding her too hard right now. Plus, starvation had a way of messing with your mind.

His jaw clenched at the weight she'd lost. She couldn't hold out much longer. Despite what he told her, he'd be force-feeding her along with Doc and Matt if she didn't start eating. He'd only said the things he'd said to get her to react. There was something about him that riled her. And he hated it.

He could see the loathing and hatred every time he entered her room. But it was the fear that he hated the most. He'd done that, but with good reason. She was the enemy, despite what the others said. Her people had been killing his for centuries, and he wouldn't risk his family and friends for a blond girl, no matter how appealing she was.

CHAPTER SEVENTEEN

Hazel

She hardly noticed Noah's departure or the door locking behind him as she stared at the blade. She scanned the room, searching for any hidden enemies, then reached out and snatched the knife from her bed. Cradling it in her palm, she squinted at it. Why give this to her? It didn't make any sense. Unless ... he didn't believe she could harm him with it. A smug smile lifted the corner of her lips as she tucked her prize underneath her pillow. That was his first mistake, underestimating her.

Hazel stared at the ceiling as the light faded to nothing, mulling over the monster's abrupt and somewhat disturbing visit. She hated to admit it, but the monster did make a good point. What would death accomplish? *Nothing.* The answer disturbed her. They hadn't physically hurt her yet. Doc didn't seem like a bad person, and Matt ... well, Matt was ... still Matt.

The darkness pressed against her as the sun fled across the sky, her little window darkening. Her eyes adjusted to the light slowly, and she stared at the one star she could see. What she wouldn't give to be outside. She missed the sun on her skin, the wind on her face as she sat on the high wall surrounding Harbor, the stars sparkling above as her brothers bickered. A lump formed in her throat. She missed home.

Hazel hadn't allowed herself to think much about home, fearing it would break her if she did. What if she never made it home? If she'd been standing, the thought would've brought her to her knees. How could she live in a world without her brothers? Without her papa? Tears flowed down her cheeks, as silent as the nighttime around her. She missed them so much it hurt.

But there wasn't just pain; there was a world of happiness. The way Brent always made room for her on the couch. How Joseph had made a game out of scaring her but always left little treasures in her room as an apology when she wouldn't speak to him afterwards. How her papa had taught her how to braid her hair even though his fingers were as clumsy as hers.

In those memories, she found strength. Her family wasn't her weakness. They were her biggest strength. They would help her survive whatever the future held, and they would be what she fought for. She *would* get back to them.

Wiping her cheeks, she smiled and began plotting. Her jailers planned to let her outside. The outdoors meant freedom, escape.

Escape.

The word sounded too big. Dangerous. A dream.

There were so many obstacles in her way. Even if she could get out of her cell, she had to get away from her captors, and once she got away from her captors, how did she find supplies? And once she found supplies, how would she get past both fences? And if she managed that, how would she know how to get home? Or survive the scary creatures and the other Tainted out there?

Hazel pulled in a deep breath to calm her racing heart and laced her fingers across her stomach. Inch by inch. She'd take it one day at a time. She couldn't race into this plan. If she did, it would be over as soon as it started. Doc, Matt, and the monster weren't stupid. They'd see right through her. If she wanted to get out of this place, she'd have to play her part perfectly.

"Hazel Bresh, so help me, you'll eat this soup."

She hid her smile as Matt stormed in the next morning wielding soup and a spoon. She scowled at him and savored his surprise as she swiped the spoon from him and almost spilled the soup.

He eyed her suspiciously as she lifted the first bite to her mouth as if he thought she might throw the bowl at him. After her next two bites, the tension fled his shoulders and he slumped into the chair, his alien eyes flickering between the spoon and her mouth.

"Stop staring," she growled.

"I can't help it. After your behavior, I expected to deal with a shrew."

Hazel glared at him and placed the leftover soup between her legs, her stomach cramping painfully. She'd only eaten half of the soup, but it was threatening to make a second appearance. If she puked, could she hit Matt from here? She grinned at the thought.

Matt's tight-lipped smile pulled her from her thoughts.

"That's the first time I've seen your smile in over a year."

Immediately, she stopped grinning.

He stood and plucked the bowl from the bed, ignoring her reaction. "I'm glad you're eating."

"I was hungry."

He snorted. "Clearly, on the account you've been starving yourself. Doc says you haven't eaten anything substantial in a week."

"Doc shouldn't be talking about my business."

"He cares about you."

She scoffed. "He cares about my worth."

"I care about you."

His words were so heartfelt and sincere that sorrow ripped through her and left her cold. She'd mourned her friend. "You should leave." The words were hollow and unexpected; they just came out.

His hurt rippled across his face before it disappeared, replaced with a familiar gleam in his eyes that she didn't like. It was one she'd seen many times growing up. Matt was about to either lose his temper or be blunt.

"You can't avoid me, Hazel. You can't pretend the past hasn't happened. Stop being so stubborn and talk to me."

"What makes you think I would want anything to do with you? My friend died." Even saying the words hurt.

"I'm right here."

She shook her head. "My Matt died. I mourned him." Her jaw clenched as her voice broke; tears thickened and clogged her throat.

"I'm right here, baby. I'm here."

He reached out to touch her hand, but she shifted out of his reach. "I don't know you. My Matt would've never left me alone."

His lips thinned, and she tried not to flinch; the corners of his fangs were slightly visible. "There's so much you don't understand. I couldn't come to you."

That hurt. "You say can't. I say won't."

Matt smiled at her, but it was more of a baring of teeth. "And you would've welcomed me with your arms wide open?" He gestured to his face. "You flinch every time I smile at you and won't let me touch you."

"It's not because of how you look." Well, for the most part.

"Are you serious? You can lie better than that."

"You know I can't." She was a terrible liar.

"I do," he said seriously. "Better than anyone."

"You did," she said softly. She'd changed a lot since his death.

He threw his hands in the air and then ran them through his hair, a heartbreakingly familiar gesture. "I don't understand. I thought you'd be as happy to see me as I am you. It's a miracle we've ended up in the same place."

"A miracle?" she whispered. "How can you even say that? I've been kidnapped, attacked by man, beast, and Tainted." He winced at her use of the word Tainted, but she continued on. "I'm in a bloody prison, Matty." As soon as the nickname came out, she wanted to take it back. It was too familiar.

"You called me Matty. I missed that."

She stared blankly at him for a moment as her emotions bubbled and churned before detonating. "I missed you! I missed you as I planned your funeral. I missed you as I placed flowers at your grave. I missed you sitting on the porch with me. I missed your smile, your humor, your kindness. I felt like it was me that had died some days. Like I wasn't even myself, because you had taken a part of me."

Her grief welled up, so acute and painful that she

could barely breathe.

"I cried myself to sleep for months. You were my best friend, my other half. And then, one day, you were just gone. Everyone continued on like the world hadn't just shifted beneath their feet. Like the world still made sense. But nothing made sense," she choked out.

"I'm so sorry," he said, his eyes gleaming. "Haz, you know I would never do anything to hurt you intentionally. I love you."

Hazel furiously swiped at her wet cheeks, his words almost breaking her, but they weren't enough. Talk was cheap, and actions spoke louder than words. His actions had proved that he didn't care *enough*. "I appreciate the words, but..."

"But it doesn't change anything," he said grimly, lines bracketing his mouth as he frowned.

She glanced away from the utter destruction rippling across his face to the dull light that filtered through the tiny window to her left, ignoring the guilt that pricked her at hurting her best friend. But she couldn't lie to him about this. She wasn't the girl he'd left behind, and he wasn't the boy she'd buried and loved.

"Hazel, I don't know what to say..." His voice broke,

and she squeezed her eyes shut at the hitch in his breathing. "I don't know how to make this right. Tell me how I can make this right."

Drawing in a deep breath, she turned to him. "We can't change the past, Matt."

His expression crumpled further. "What is this hell?" he whispered.

"It's life," she whispered back.

Hazel stared at her old friend for a long moment, hating that she couldn't trust him, hating that he'd left her, and hating that he hadn't hugged her and said everything would be alright. Her emotions were confounding.

Not able to bear the pain on his face any longer, she blurted, "Life is crap and then we die, but friends last a lifetime. You've hurt me, and we can't go back to what we were."

Matt's shoulders slumped further, but he pasted on a sardonic grin. "Other than the obvious?" He gestured to his fangs and slitted, snake-like eyes.

"Among other things," she murmured. "Even though we can't change the past, it's not easily forgotten. And I don't want to forget." Her eyes began to burn again.

"They were good times," he said, smiling.

"The best," she agreed. All her favorite memories had Matt in them. That wasn't something to take lightly, despite his abandonment. She shoved her hand out abruptly between them. Matt blinked at it and then glanced to her face. "I propose a new start."

Another blink.

She cleared her throat and glared at her arm as it began to tremble. She'd lost so much strength in such little time. "I'm Hazel."

Matt's smile started small and widened, exposing all of his teeth as if he was testing her. Hazel didn't flinch back or waver. She was made of stronger stuff. She was like her mother. A relieved puff of breath passed her lips as he reached out and shook her hand slowly.

"I'm Matt."

"What large teeth you have," she muttered, smiling slightly.

He released her hand, his eyes glittering with mirth. "How long have you been waiting to use that?"

"Since I saw your teeth."

Chuckling, he slapped his knees and then reached out to cradle her hand between his. "I'll always be your friend." He sighed. "There are things we need to talk about."

He always had to push. At least, that wasn't something new. "Not now…" She sighed. Her eyelids felt so heavy. The conversation had exhausted her.

"You can't hide from the truth."

She pulled her hand from his and rubbed at her eyes. "When have I ever hid from the truth?"

"Never, but then again, you claim that you're not the same girl I used to know."

"Can't this be enough for now?" Hazel stared blurrily in his direction.

Matt studied her, then nodded. "For now."

"Now, get out," she commanded as she scooted down into the bed.

"You always were grumpy when you got tired."

"Everyone's grumpy when they're tired." She yawned and snuggled into her pillow, her eyes drifting closed. "Name one person who's happy and chipper when they're tired," she murmured.

"You've got me there." The chair creaked as he stood. She stilled as he pressed a kiss to the crown of her head. "Sleep well, babe. I'll see you later."

Hazel didn't respond and kept her eyes closed until the door closed behind him and she could no longer hear his footsteps. Dust motes danced in the air as she curled her hand around the blade hidden underneath her pillow.

Everything she'd said to Matt was the truth. She'd meant every word, and yet ... guilt nagged at her. Hazel had never been one to hold grudges. He'd hurt her, but eventually, the wound would heal like they all did, and she'd move on. But making peace with Matt served two purposes this time. One, he deserved a second chance; and two, she wasn't going to stay in this hole forever.

And Matt? Well, he was her ticket to escape.

CHAPTER EIGHTEEN

Hazel

It was almost comical to see how startled Doc was when he entered the room. The door thumped against the wall as he gaped at her. Hazel blushed and patted at her hair. She'd done the best she could to braid the rat's nest.

"Is it that bad?" she asked.

He snapped his mouth shut and moved into the room with lithe grace. "You look lovely."

Hazel snorted. "Even I know I look like roadkill."

Doc grinned over his shoulder as he unpacked the bag full of medical supplies. The smell of fresh bread filled the room, and her mouth began to water as he pulled two wrapped packages out of the bag.

"I thought you'd like something other than broth this morning," he said cheerily.

She swore drool rolled down her chin as he handed her the thick slice of bread covered in butter. "That smells amazing." Memories of her mama bustling around the kitchen while she sat on the counter sneaking berries and bread crumbs from the cutting board slammed into her. "Thank you," she said, taking a deep bite. "Oh my gosh, this is so good."

Doc coughed and rubbed the back of his neck, smiling wryly. "Do you want me to give you some alone time with the bread?"

Hazel rolled her eyes and took another bite, groaning. "Don't judge me. It's so good."

"I'll tell Noah you said so."

She froze, the bread turning to ash in her mouth. The monster had made the bread?

Doc scowled. "Stop looking like you're going to drop dead any moment. Do you think I'd let him poison one of my patients?"

It wasn't that she thought the monster would kill her. It was more that she didn't want to touch anything he'd touched, let alone put it in her body.

"You eat all of that," Doc said sternly, his amber

eyes glinting. "If you don't, well ... I won't take you to the baths."

"Baths?" What wouldn't she give for a proper bath? She squinted, trying to remember how long it had been. Six weeks? Maybe longer? She didn't even know how long she'd been in this cell. But the one thing she knew for sure was the sponge baths weren't cutting it anymore. She peeked at the pot in the corner. The pee pot was getting old too.

Slowly, she took another bite and chewed while staring Doc down. She'd eat everything the monster made if it meant she could escape this room. He quirked a smile and sat on the bed.

"Left hand."

Obediently, she held her left hand out for his inspection while systematically eating her bread, even though she didn't have much of an appetite left. His auburn hair fell forward, shielding his eyes, his ears twitching with each of her movements as he checked her abused wrists. They'd scar, for sure, but at least she was alive.

Shame welled up inside her; she shoved it down ruthlessly, so the bread wouldn't make a second appearance after she finished the last bite. Fear did something to a person. She'd made the right choice now, and that was brave.

His right ear twitched again, and an involuntary giggle slipped out. Doc glanced up from his work, his amber eyes peeking at her from beneath his fringe of hair.

"What's so funny?"

"Nothing."

"Sure," he drawled, returning to his work.

His ears looked so soft and cute. They kind of made her want to pet him. Without thought, she reached her right hand out and touched the tip of his ear. Doc froze but didn't recoil. Fascinated at the silky texture, she ran her fingers over the deep red fur covering his ears. "So soft," she whispered.

Doc let her explore and then slowly pulled her hand from his hair. Mortification swamped her as she saw the expression on his face. It was one part amused, one part hot. He pressed a kiss to the back of her hand and gave her a roguish smile.

"I feel that I should warn you that you've officially moved into mating ground."

"Mating what?" she blurted.

He waved his left hand toward his ears. "Women only ever touch a man's ears if she's interested in being his life partner."

"Life partner?" she squeaked. "I wasn't—"

"I know," he hushed her. "As titillating as that experience was, I don't believe kits are in our future, and I wanted you to become comfortable with me."

She shook her head hard, her messy braid swinging in the air. "No kits." What a weird way of saying *children*. "I'm sorry for getting into your personal space."

He smiled at her gently and patted her arm. "Don't worry about it. Right hand."

Hazel watched at he pulled the gauze from her right wrist. "You have very nice ears," she said awkwardly. "They suit you."

Doc chuckled. "Thank you, Hazel. I'm glad you like them."

"Is that the only thing that's different...?"

He smeared a pungent salve across her wrist and began wrapping it again. "The ears are the only visible change to my body. My sight and hearing are better than an Untouched."

"Untouched?" she asked.

"Someone who's not been blessed with the change."

"You mean human."

Doc tied the gauze and stared at her hard. "Am I not

human?"

That wasn't a question she'd let herself think about. "I don't know what you are."

"When I look at you, I see a strong, brave girl who's been through some bad situations and has succeeded despite fear and heartbreak. What do you see when you look at me?"

What did she see? Doc had treated her with care and concern since she'd arrived, even though she'd treated him poorly. "I see a kind, generous soul who cares for the needs of others."

"Neither of us described how each other physically look. Why should our appearances have anything to do with how human we are? It's what we do that shows how much humanity we have."

His words rang true. Aaron's face flashed through her mind. She'd met her fair share of monsters that wore a human face. "That we agree on. I was never one to judge a book by its cover, but you have to admit" – she waved a hand at the room – "all of this is a little much. And not all of you are human by your standards." The winged monster would never be human in her mind.

"Don't allow prejudice to take root in your heart."

Prejudice. What an ugly word. She'd seen it

growing up and it always sickened her. The color of one's skin did not matter. The way a person dressed did not matter. A person's prominence didn't matter. All that mattered was what kind of person you were. That's what Hazel looked at, anyhow. Then why was it so hard to think that way when it came to the Tainted? "Is Untouched a slur like Tainted?"

Doc winced. "Yes and No. It depends who you're talking to."

"The monster didn't like it."

"I'm sure Noah didn't. He's a sensitive sort."

Hazel huffed out a breath. "That I highly doubt."

"What was that about judging a book by its cover?" Doc murmured, arching a brow.

"I'm not judging him by his looks. I'm judging him by his actions." A fissure of fear went down her spine at the way he'd threatened her before.

Doc cocked his head, his eyes narrowing. "What has he done?"

"Nothing," she whispered. What could Doc do for her? Nothing. What the monster threatened didn't matter.

He pushed from the bed and hastily scooped his supplies back into his bag, startling her. "I'm going to put these back in the infirmary, and then I'll come get you for that bath." He smiled at her and then was gone.

Hazel stared at the door. What in the blazes had just happened?

CHAPTER NINETEEN

Noah

He could smell Doc's anger before his friend stormed into the infirmary. Noah crossed his arms and watched in silence as the kitsune tossed his bag onto the cot with more force than necessary.

"What's got you so angry?" he asked as Doc paced the red dirt room.

Doc whirled, his amber eyes turned to slits. "You," he growled. "You're despicable."

Noah chuckled. *How unoriginal.* "That's nothing new. Would you remind me of what I did this time? It's hard to keep up."

Doc's face darkened to a deep shade of red. "You

threatened her."

Understanding dawned. The little Untouched viper had obviously been filling the kitsune's head with stories. "She's spinning tales, is she?"

"No, she wouldn't say a damn thing, but I could smell her fear. Fear that she only has when you're mentioned. What did you do, Noah?"

Guilt and shame tried to rise up at how he'd acted when she first arrived, but he ruthlessly shoved it down into the box of emotions he didn't want to deal with and slammed the lid closed. There was no need to feel guilty over his actions. He was ensuring the safety of his people. Plus, he'd already told the girl that he didn't mean it. It was her choice not to believe him.

"I protected our people," he said at last.

"Is that what you're telling yourself?" Doc sneered. "What a pretty little lie."

Noah glared at his friend. "You know our people come first. She's a stranger. Untouched. Dangerous."

"Right," Doc drawled, "'cause that slip of a girl looks like a real killer. One can't be too careful."

"Exactly. She could be a spy."

"Oh, please. From Remy and Matt's accounts, Hazel was kept ignorant of the world around her. If she's a spy for her colony, I'll eat my hat."

"You don't have a hat," Noah retorted. They bothered his friend's ears.

Doc scowled. "You've made things worse, right? She barely trusts me, and Matt's on thin ice."

"She doesn't need to trust us." Noah pushed from the wall and flexed his wings. He hated being underground. Being of the avion class, all he wanted was to feel the wind on his face and under his wings. "All she needs –" He lost his thought as a scent drifted through the air. He inhaled deeper as the hair along the nape of his neck prickled and understanding dawned. "It appears you've managed to gain quite a bit more than just trust from the girl," he bit out. He could smell the Untouched all over Doc.

"You know I have to touch my patients," Doc replied with exasperation.

"And your ears?" Noah accused, his hands curling into fists.

Doc took one look at him and swiped a scalpel from the counter to his right. "She was curious, that's all. I let her explore."

"Explore?" he murmured, hating how dark and dangerous his voice sounded.

"You're itching for a fight, but I don't want to be the

one who hands you your ass. We can't afford to destroy anything in this room."

"She touched you." *In a sexual way* was implied.

"Because she didn't know any better. I explained that to her."

"After the fact."

Doc tipped his head back and closed his eyes as if he was asking for strength. "It was the first time she's initiated contact with me. It's a step in the right direction, and I wasn't going to ruin her wonder." He opened his eyes and shrugged, a half-smile on his face. "It's been a long time since someone acted that way with me. It was a beautiful thing to behold."

"You had no right." Stupid words wouldn't stop coming out of his mouth. He sounded like a jealous lover.

Doc sighed and rolled his neck. "I have every right. I assume you came down here for another reason than to fight with me?"

"The Montgomery twins are sick. Amelia needs help caring for them."

"That's the last thing she needs, poor thing. She's due in two weeks." Doc rushed around the room, tossing an arsenal of medical supplies into his faded olive-green canvas bag. "Jake's death couldn't have been timed worse."

"Because him dying at another time would be better?" Noah asked.

"No, but soon she'll be a single mother of three. That's a life of hard work."

"Life is hard. But she's not alone. She has the entire village, and Jameson has been helping out."

Doc chuckled. "I'm sure he has, the bastard."

"He cares for her."

"If he cared for her, he'd stay far away from Amelia. I tend to his wounds every time he goes out. He's too reckless, and if he commits to her, it will be just another husband she has to bury and her children have to mourn."

"That's a bit dark for you," Noah commented.

"No, it's realistic." The kitsune checked his bag one more time, murmuring to himself, and then threw it over his shoulder with a groan. "Darn it, I told Hazel I'd take her to the baths." Doc's eyes narrowed in thought. "You'll have to take her. I have to care for the twins."

Noah scowled. "I have a council meeting in an hour."

Doc paused at his side. The kitsune was shorter than Noah's towering height, but just slightly. "Then make it quick – and be nice."

Noah grunted and followed Doc out of the infirmary. The rounded sandstone hallways were always cool and caused his skin to prickle. "Is she even strong enough to walk? I'm not carrying her."

A snort. "I don't think she'd allow you to touch her even if she wasn't." Doc turned right, leaving Noah in the hallway that led to the cells. "Oh…" The kitsune faced Noah, walking backward. "I'm not blind to what you've got going on. Just remember, it's going to be that much harder the longer you hold onto your prejudice." He spun on his heel. "Don't be an idiot," Doc called before disappearing.

"Bastard," Noah muttered to the empty hallway. He heaved a deep breath and began to stride purposefully down the hallway. Taking her to the baths wasn't a difficult task. He needed to suck it up and get the job done. He didn't have time to waste messing around.

He spotted her door and paused outside it, fishing the key from his pocket and opening the door.

The girl sat with her back to him, the light from the small window haloing her, turning her hair a bright silver. Like an angel. His jaw clenched. It wasn't right how pretty she was.

"I'm ready to go," she said excitedly. She jumped from the bed and spun around with a huge smile that promptly slid off her face, an expression of horror replacing it.

Noah hid his wince at the smell of her acrid terror. "Noah sent me. It's time for your bath." His nose wrinkled. "You stink."

Some of her fear slid away, and she straightened, glaring at him even though her hands continued to tremble. "It serves you right. You get to deal with the product of your neglect."

"Oh, please," he huffed. He turned to leave the room. "If you want a bath, I suggest you get moving."

He listened for the soft pad of footsteps as he strolled down the hallway. Her fear had dulled a little, mixed with the sharp bite of anger. He grinned as hesitant footsteps followed him. He hated the fear, but he could work with the anger.

CHAPTER TWENTY

Hazel

This was stupid.

If her brothers were here, they'd smack her on the back of her head and tell her to go back to her cell.

Hazel eyed the monster ahead of her, hating how much room he took up. His wings were massive and almost touched the curved hallway ceiling. As if he could sense she was thinking about him, he glanced over his shoulder, his black eyes catching hers for a terrifying moment. She shuddered as he focused ahead.

There was something so unnerving about him. A wry smile twisted her lips for a beat. Well, besides the wings, scales, and teeth.

Another shiver worked through her as they traipsed the hallways, the light growing fainter and fainter. She rubbed at her bare arms as unease prickled her. What if he wasn't taking her to the baths? What if he was getting rid of her? Or worse? It was the *worse* that scared her the most, but she comforted herself with the knowledge she'd gained on this little trek. Luckily for her, her captors didn't know about her uncanny ability to memorize almost anything. She'd logged all the twists and turns they'd taken. In a pinch, she could get back to her cell.

They rounded another corner, the hallway sloping downward. Hazel ran her hand along the wall for balance and her legs wobbled beneath her. Her jaw clenched, and she locked her knees. She was so weak, and she had no one to blame but her own stupid self.

She brushed her hair from her sweaty forehead and grimaced at the smell around them. It smelled like dirty socks and rotten eggs. What was that smell? She gagged and pulled the collar of her tan cotton dress over her nose. The air warmed around her to the point that it felt like she was breathing water. Her gasp was muffled as the walkway emptied into a huge room that was shaped like a beehive. Steam rose from the huge pool of turquoise water. She'd never seen water that color before. A wide walkway surrounded the entire pool, and seats were carved into the sandstone walls.

Unable to help herself, she moved toward the edge and knelt, dipping her fingers into the water. Another gasp flew past her lips. It was warm. "What is this place?" she breathed.

"The hot springs."

"Hot springs?" she repeated. She'd never heard of such a thing. Hot springs seemed too boring of a name for such a magical place.

"Yes, hot springs," the monster said, annoyance coloring his tone. "We haven't got all day to gawk." He stabbed a pointed finger toward a basket to her left. "You'll find soap in there. Be quick."

She glanced from the basket to the oddly-colored water with a frown. Was that why the water was an odd color? How many people had bathed here? She scrambled over to the basket as the monster leveled another glare at her before placing his back to her. Beggars couldn't be choosers.

There were several lumps of soap in the basket, and she experimentally sniffed one. She smiled as lavender and mint teased her nose. Scented soap was a luxury at home, but it was always something she'd made time to make. It made her feel more girly.

The smile slipped from her face, and she put her favorite soap back. Now was not the time she wanted to smell girly. Hazel sniffed each soap and chose the most masculine scent she could find. She didn't know what it was, per se, but it was earthy.

Her gaze dropped to her dress as she swung her legs into the pool, the hot water caressing her skin. She would have loved to bathe properly, but she wasn't foolish enough to actually undress when there was a predator in the room.

Her eyes practically rolled back in her head as she waded, the water rolling around at her waist.

"Keep away from the middle. It's deep."

Hazel nodded and realized he couldn't see her. "Okay." He didn't know she could swim. And she'd keep that part to herself. The less he knew about her the better. But it didn't stop the longing that bombarded her. She loved to swim. Her mama had always told her she was part fish. Hazel didn't like to think she was like one of the slimy fishes she'd hated to eat, so as a child she'd pretended she was part mermaid, a mythical creature she'd read about in the books.

But the worst part was the sun. The cavern arched up above the direct center of the pool into a flute that let in one beam of sunlight. Her eyes closed as she imagined the sun on her skin. She wiggled her toes in the soft sand, tiny smooth rocks rolling beneath her feet. Those were dreams for another day. She'd see the sun again. She'd be free.

"Tick tock."

Hazel's eyes snapped open, the dream shattered, and made a face. The monster ruined everything. She tipped her head back, wetting her hair. Her brows furrowed as she stared at the contraption that hung from the ceiling. It looked like an old wagon wheel. She blinked and then began to scrub vigorously at every bit of skin she could reach as she realized what It was. Sometimes, she was so clueless. It was a light. But how did it work? She scoured the cave. She couldn't see any wires. So, either it was solar-powered or it was an old relic.

"Five minutes."

Jerk. He seemed to take pleasure in being a brute.

She glanced in his direction while placing the soap on the stone edge and rinsing her hair and body. Well, if she had five minutes, she certainly wasn't getting out yet. Hazel pulled in a deep breath and slowly sank into the water. A sense of calm surrounded her in the utter silence. That was what she loved the most about swimming. The peace. The quiet.

She popped up for another breath and then sank deeper; her fingers touched the sand and rocks, and she braved opening her eyes. It was utterly beautiful. The stones gleamed like they were polished in every color. Hazel spotted two bigger rocks and drifted toward them. She spun on to her back, her hair dancing in the current as she wrapped her hands around the rocks, so she wouldn't float back to the surface.

She'd always been fascinated with mythical creatures from a young age, but mermaids were her favorite. Her mama brought her many mermaids from her scav trips and Hazel still had each one. As a little girl, she'd pretended that the red sand surrounding the compound were rippling waves but none of that could compare to this cove. Hazel smiled, small bubbles floating from her mouth. This was as close to being a mermaid as she'd ever get.

The sun danced across the water, sending ripples of light to the bottom. She closed her eyes, her lungs uncomfortable but not screaming yet. She'd stay here as long as she could before she braved the scary world above.

The sunlight disappeared, and a body slammed into her. Hazel's eyes popped open and she screamed, bubbles streaming from her mouth. The monster wrapped an arm around her waist and jerked her upward. She sucked in a breath and choked as water rushed into her mouth.

Pain exploded from her chest as they broke the surface. Rough stone met her chest, and then a hand slammed between her shoulder blades. Water spewed from her throat as she coughed and heaved until there was no more.

Tears streamed down her face as she leaned a cheek against the edge of the pool. She'd almost drowned.

"Did you really think I'd let you drown yourself?" the monster spat, every word holding an edge of violence and contempt.

He thought she was trying to drown herself? Ire burned through her and she slapped at his arms, not caring how the scales on his forearms caused goosebumps on hers. She hauled herself out of the pool onto shaking legs and glared at him.

"*You* were the one who almost drowned *me*! I was just fine."

Her captor pushed his black hair from his face and pulled himself from the pool, water streaming from his wings and wet torso. She scowled as he stood to his full height and leaned toward her, utterly intimidating. It was times like these that she wished she were a few inches taller.

"Do you remember what I said about lying?" he asked, deceptively soft.

"I'm not lying," she gritted out, and placed her hands on her hips. "I was enjoying a peaceful moment until you jumped on me." Hazel waved a hand at him. "If you want to blame anyone, blame yourself."

He growled at her and crossed his arms, glancing away from her in disgust. "Let's go." A pause. "You might want to think about covering up. I'm assured there's no one down here that you can use your feminine wiles on."

"Feminine wiles, what in the Sam Hill are you...?" She broke off as she twisted the water from her dress. Her dress.

Horror, embarrassment, and shame battled each other as she saw what state her dress was in. The water had made it see-through. Completely and utterly see-through. She might as well have been naked for all the good it did her. "Do you have a towel?" She hated that she had to ask him for anything, but she'd throw her pride away if it meant she could cover herself from his mocking gaze.

He spun and yanked a brown towel from another basket. She kept her face blank as he threw it at her. It was a hand towel. "What do you expect me to do with this?"

"Dry yourself."

A hollow laugh escaped her. So, he meant to shame her. Well, she'd get the last laugh. Hazel rang out her dress and then wrapped the tiny towel around her neck. "Lead on," she said sarcastically.

He glowered at her and marched past her. Hazel followed and crossed her arms over her chest while his back was turned, not believing she'd done that. She shook her head and took one last look at the hot springs before scurrying to catch up with her jailer from hell.

The steady drip of water from the monster ahead of her was the only sound as they trekked back to her cell. By the time her door came in sight, she was almost relieved. She was exhausted, and her throat burned.

The monster held open her door but didn't enter. She paused for a moment, and then squared her shoulders. Yes, she'd have to squeeze past him to get inside her cell, but he'd already been pressed up against her today and seen her naked. A hysterical laugh threatened to make its appearance as she skirted by him, her skin barely brushing his. Hazel jerked and spun around to see the door closing. The soft snick of the lock registered as she plopped on the bed and stared at nothing.

She could've sworn he'd touched her hair.

CHAPTER TWENTY-ONE

Noah

He was an idiot.

Noah stood outside her door, staring at his hand like it was a traitor.

He'd touched her. Reached out and caressed her hair like she wasn't an Untouched, like she was *his* to touch.

He hissed and jogged away from her door, his wet jeans rubbing uncomfortably against his hips. It wasn't like he hadn't seen a pretty girl before. The image of her glaring at him, soaking wet, flashed through his mind.

"Dang it," he growled underneath his breath. She

was more than pretty. She was stunning. And off-limits, no matter what others said. He had to keep himself above reproach. His attraction to the girl wasn't acceptable.

He checked his watch and his left wrist. He was going to be late. Wonderful. And he didn't even have time to change his clothes. Noah took a sniff of himself, his frown deepened. Not only was he going to be late, but he was going in there smelling of the girl, aggression, and arousal. Just perfect.

CHAPTER TWENTY-TWO

Hazel

Hazel sat in Doc's usual chair, watching the light slowly fade from her window. He'd arrive with dinner soon and start scolding her.

Her dress lay over her bare bed, drying in the day's last rays of sun. She ran her fingers over the sheet dress she'd created as she thought over the last couple of hours.

Hazel had fallen asleep as soon as she had yanked her dress off and hopped into bed. But what was more notable was her discovery upon waking. As she'd stared at her ceiling, thinking about the pool, she'd realized something life-changing. She'd seen the sun.

A way out. Until today, she'd no idea of how to escape the labyrinth of tunnels. But now, she did. She had her exit, and a plan.

It was simple, really. Drug Matt, steal the sheet, and get to the pool. Once she was there, she'd create a rope of sorts, tie a rock on one side, and throw it up and over the wagon wheel light. The light was way too high for her to jump to, but she could climb to it. As for the flute, well, it was just wide enough that she could climb it. She'd climbed things like that before, although if she slipped this time, she'd die.

It was possible. She could do it. All she needed was another five days.

Her stomach cramped, and she winced. She needed to get stronger, and she didn't want to try to escape while during her moon time. Not only would that be dumb, but miserable as well.

The door swung open, pulling her from her thoughts as Doc stalked in with his doc face on. She held up her hands. "I see he's gotten to you with his side of the story. Are you willing to listen to mine?"

He shut the door and passed her a bowl of soup and a thick slice of bread, then crashed on her bed, his arm flung over his face. "Lay it on me."

"I was bathing,"

"Obviously."

"Anyhow," she said over his comment, "I was enjoying my bath and there were some beautiful rocks that I wanted to see. Underneath the water is so quiet and peaceful. It's a break from reality."

Doc sighed and sat up, his red hair sticking up in every direction. "So, you weren't trying to kill yourself?"

"No." She held his gaze steadily, so he'd see she wasn't lying.

"Good," he said at last. "I don't have time for a crazy patient."

"Speaking of patients..." she drew out.

"What?" he asked.

"I need some things."

"Some ... things," he said slowly. "You need to clarify. I can't read minds."

"It's my moon time," she blurted.

Doc blinked at her. His nose twitched, and he wiped at it, his expression blank. "Not sure how I missed that."

Heat rushed into her cheeks. "And how would you know that?"

"Not important." He sprang to his feet and dashed for the door. "You eat your food and I'll be back with what you need." The door began to close, and then he popped his head back in. "Cramps, nausea, headaches?"

"All of it." Truly, the cramps were the only things bothering her, but whatever he brought with him would be helpful for when she was on the run. "And..."

"What?" he asked gently.

"I'm having a hard time sleeping."

One nod and he was gone. Hazel slurped her soup down and then munched on her bread, waiting for him. When he came back, he had an arsenal with him. He spread it out on the bed and explained what each thing did.

"Thank you," she said, feeling awful for taking advantage of his generosity and care. "Really, I mean it."

"I know," he said, patting her hand. He scooped up her spoon and bowl and threw his pack over his shoulder. "I'll see you in the morning."

"Alright. Sleep well."

He smiled at her and swung open the door. "You too, Hazel."

The waiting was killing her.

Three days passed in a blur of bread, cramps, and

boredom.

The problem was, being healthier meant she slept less, and that left more time to sit and stew about her circumstances. And her escape.

She glanced around the small room as if someone could read her thoughts. If she made one mistake, her escape would go up in flames.

The snick of the lock pulled her from her thoughts. She swung her feet over the bed to wait for Matt. He'd taken to visiting her every evening, leaving after she fell asleep. She didn't know what to make of that, but regardless, it was a welcome comfort to have someone watching over her who wasn't the enemy.

The door swung open and two unfamiliar Tainted stepped into the room. Hazel rolled off the bed to put the furniture between her and them. Her hand slid underneath the pillow and wrapped around the smooth handle of the knife there.

Silence teeming with violence filled the room as they stared at each other. The small Tainted was a woman. Hazel's eyes were immediately drawn to her leathery wings. They were angular, kind of like the woman herself. She was so tiny, she made Hazel look like a giant. With a little envy, she gazed at the woman's bronze skin. It was obvious she had Spanish descent and spent time in the sun. *Lucky.*

Hazel pulled her gaze away from the Spanish beauty to focus on the man. He was huge, wide-shouldered, and had thick arms and legs. She swallowed at the black and yellow scales that ran along his arms and disappeared into his t-shirt. His hawkish cheekbones melded with more scales, and with difficulty, she met his hard stare.

He gave nothing away and stared back. Despite his calm demeanor, it was like he wore a cape of danger around him.

"Well, you're not Matt." The statement cut some of the tension.

The man smiled, flashing her a mouthful of sharper teeth, but blessedly no fangs.

"We aren't."

The woman's voice was raspy and deep, completely opposite of her appearance. Hazel glanced at the woman, noting she had soft, fawn-like eyes. "I'd normally welcome you, but since these are not normal circumstances, I'll be blunt. Who are you and what are you doing in my cell?"

"Technically, it's our cell," the male retorted.

You've got to be kidding me. "So, I owe my imprisonment to you?" she asked carefully, her tone giving nothing away.

"Something like that," the woman muttered, eyeing Hazel like she could pull her apart and figure out what made her tick. "We've been remiss in our duties in visiting."

"In visiting your prisoner?" Hazel said in confusion.

"In visiting the newest member of our village," the man said. He gestured to the chair. "Do you mind if I sit? My back is killing me."

Hazel nodded, her brows furrowed as she tried to make sense of what the devil was going on. She shook her head. "I think you're mistaken. I'm not of your village."

"That's where you're wrong, Untouched," the woman said. "It's been discussed with the council, and with our approval, they've decided to allow you to stay."

"Stay?" Hazel asked stupidly. She couldn't have heard her right.

"There was much debate on what to do with you. You're valuable. We would gain much wealth if we sold you ... but we're not slavers." The disgust at the idea of slaves was palpable from his tone. "Others believed we should make sport of you."

Hazel shifted on her feet and lifted her blade

higher. "No one will make sport of me."

The man shifted his massive bulk in the chair, crossing his ankle over a thick thigh. Amusement sparkled in his eyes. "Of that, I have no doubt. I've heard whisperings that you've been trouble down here. Are you trouble?"

"Only if you intend to harm me. If you leave me alone, I'll leave you alone."

His gaze wandered to the blade, and he shook his head, mumbling something. The woman's fawn eyes sharpened on the blade she held, a noise gurgling in the back of her throat.

Hazel cleared her throat. "I don't intend to harm you ... as long as you don't plan to harm me," she reiterated.

"How did you come by that blade?" the woman murmured.

Hazel allowed herself a grin. They were concerned about the blade. Maybe the monster would pay for some of his mistakes. "A monster gave it to me. I think he expected me to end my life with it."

At her use of *monster*, both Tainted stiffened. "Is that how you see us, as monsters?" the male asked softly.

They certainly looked like monsters, but ... they

hadn't hurt her, and they hadn't sold her into slavery. That meant they weren't awful people, but there was no guarantee they were innocent.

"You've given me no proof that you are, but I reserve the right to judgement."

The woman laughed softly. "You're an interesting one." A glance at the male. "I can see her appeal."

He hummed and scanned Hazel head-to-toe in a look that didn't feel sexual, just assessing. "Our son doesn't trust you."

"Your son?" Her nose wrinkled as she glanced between them. She didn't know their son. The only Tainted she'd met since arriving were … realization slammed into her and she stumbled back against the wall, cold seeping through her cotton dress. These were the monster's parents. She knew they reminded her of someone.

"We're not here to hurt you, Hazel," the male soothed.

They knew her name? She wanted to slap herself. Of course, they knew her name.

The woman stepped forward, her wings rustling behind her. "My name is Sara, and this is my husband Clint. We're the ruling couple of the classes here in the Arch."

"Classes?" Hazel muttered.

"Lessons for another time," Clint said, pushing from his chair. "Today, all you need to know is that your incarceration ends tomorrow. We'll find you a place to live and assign you a job."

Slave labor.

He opened the door and nodded to Hazel. "It was nice to meet you."

Sara paused by the door, her shrewd eyes softening. "Don't be fearful. Tomorrow marks the first day of the rest of your life."

Hazel stood in place long after the couple had left. They'd messed with her plan. They were going to move her from here to another prison. She had no doubt that was what it would be. The couple spouted pretty lies. Oh, they hadn't sold her, but it was for their own selfish gain.

They'd raised the monster, so by all rights, they were monsters, too.

She'd have to escape tonight.

CHAPTER TWENTY-THREE

Hazel

"How are you feeling today?"

Hazel rolled her eyes as she fiddled with the frayed edge of the blanket lying across her lap. "The same as every day, I suppose." She glanced at him from the corner of her eye. "You've asked that for the last three days."

Matt shrugged and leaned his head back against the chair, staring at the ceiling. "I'm just worried about you."

"I wasn't trying to hurt myself." She'd told him that every day, and yet, she got the feeling he didn't believe her. "Why don't you believe me?"

"It's not that I don't believe you, but..." He hesitated. "Babe, you were a mess when Noah let me in. I can't get the images out of my mind." He ran a hand over his mouth. "There was so much blood. I have nightmares."

She cringed. "It wasn't about you. None of it was. I was trying to escape."

He glanced at her. "By starving yourself? By cutting yourself over and over?" He shuddered. "Forgive me for being overprotective and skeptical. Your actions spoke plainly of your motives."

Hazel glanced away, gazing at the shadows the warm lantern light cast against the wall. This conversation wasn't going the way she needed it to. She needed him pliant, not argumentative.

"Do you remember the sleepovers we had as children?" His breath hitched, but she didn't look his way. "Sleeping in front of the fireplace, shadow puppets, my mama reading us stories..."

"I miss those days," Matt said roughly.

So did she. Hazel grinned when a shadow bird appeared on the wall, all lopsided and wonky. "That's pathetic."

"Well, it's been years. I dare you to do better."

Smiling, she twisted her fingers into a rough rabbit shape. "Beat that."

The shadow puppet war began. By the end, they were both laughing so hard they couldn't breathe. She grabbed her chest and straightened, wiping her eyes. "That was terrible."

Matt held up a finger with a grin. "Just to be clear, I won."

She snorted. "You won the lamest shadow puppet award."

"Har har," he retorted. "You were just as bad."

Hazel sniffed and picked up her cup from next to her bed, swirling the contents. Mint and lavender curled around her. "Thanks," she whispered, glancing over the rim and pretending to take a drink. "That was fun."

His smile gentled and he reached out to clasp her right hand. "It was. It felt like I had my old friend back."

Her stomach sank. He'd never get his old friend back. That Hazel was gone for good. She glanced at her cup again, trying to ignore the guilt at what she was about to do.

"I'm different now, Matty."

"I know. Things have changed between us."

She glanced at him, only able to hold his gaze for a moment before staring at her lap. "More than you know." She swallowed. "I have nightmares."

"Of what?"

"Monsters, death, and pain." The words tasted bitter on her tongue. They were the truth, but she didn't wish to share them with him. They were a manipulation to get her way. Truth or not, it still made her a traitor.

"I've been having a hard time sleeping, but thankfully Doc's been giving me something to help with that." She gave him a half smile and held the cup out to him. "You might give it a try. It might help with your nightmares."

He glanced thoughtfully at the cup she held out. "I tend to stay away from Doc's teas. They're usually disgusting."

Hazel barked out a laugh. Matt wasn't far from the truth, but this one was sweet, and Matty had always had a weakness for sweets. "True, but..." She glanced around like she was about to tell a secret. "Doc snagged some honey for me. It's so sweet."

Matt's eyes narrowed. "He made you sweet tea? That bastard." He waved his fingers at her. "Hand that over."

She did, watching with chagrin at his deep sip. He held it back out to her, and she waved a hand at him. "I've had enough. Feel free to drink the rest." She snuggled into her bed and turned onto her side to stare at him as he drank the rest.

"You ready for bed, babe?" he asked, placing the cup on the floor.

"Yeah, it's been a long day." She laughed. "Even though I haven't done anything."

"Your body needs time to heal, and sleep is the best thing for that." He scooched down in the chair and smiled at her. "I'll stay 'til you fall asleep."

Blinking away the tears in her eyes, she reached a hand out from underneath the covers. Matt blinked at her and reached out to hold it.

"Thank you for being here for me. It means a lot." *Please forgive me.*

He squeezed her hand and yawned. "This is our second chance, Hazel. We're lucky we found each other again. It just proves that nothing can break friendships that were meant to last a lifetime."

Except death. "Best friends?" she asked.

"Always," he answered.

She released his hand and hunkered down in the bed, pretending her best to be falling asleep, even though her entire body was lit up with nerves.

Matt turned the lantern down and then wiggled around in his chair until he got comfortable. She crushed the blankets between her fingers as he slowly nodded off, and his breathing deepened.

She waited an hour and it was excruciating. "Matt?" she whispered.

Nothing.

Hazel sat up and swung her legs over the side of the bed. "Matt," she said louder.

Still nothing.

Her shoulders slumped. Doc's sleeping draught had done its job.

She tiptoed from the bed, pulling the sheet with her. She'd torn off a section earlier that day and created a rough knapsack to carry the supplies Doc had left with her. Hazel paused at the foot of the bed and scanned the cell that had been her home for weeks. Her lot could have been worse.

Finally, she turned toward Matt and moved to his side. In sleep, he still looked like the boy she grew up with, the one she'd loved. They'd never been *in love* with each other, but she was his, just as he was hers, and that wouldn't ever change. He was right; they had a friendship people dreamed about. Unable to help herself, she pressed a kiss to his cheek, his rough sandy five o'clock shadow abrading her lips.

Again, nothing. He didn't stir.

Hazel pulled herself from her friend, taking the keys he kept in the front pocket of his shirt, and snuck toward the door. She inhaled deeply and stole one last look at her friend before opening the door. Her nerves sang as she peeked out into the dark hallway, lit only by little puddles of moonlight here and there. The coast was clear.

She shut the door quietly behind her, locked the door, then listened for any sounds. It was like the world was holding its breath. Her hands shook as she shoved the keys into her bra. This was it. It was now or never.

Hazel strode down the hallway as fast as she could without running, avoiding the puddles of moonlight. She was thankful for her sharp memory at that moment. After three left turns and a right and another left, the smell of rotten eggs assaulted her. So close.

A humming echoed from the hot springs, causing Hazel to skid to a stop. *Dang it.* She'd hoped there wouldn't be anyone in here at this time of night. Carefully, she pulled a small but stout metal bar from her knapsack. Thank goodness for old metal beds.

She crept forward and peered through the steam. Her heart sank as she caught a familiar auburn head of hair.

Doc.

Of all the stupid luck.

Hazel squeezed her eyes closed. She couldn't hurt him after he'd helped her so much. What was she supposed to do? Did she run back to her cell and pretend none of this happened? No. She opened her eyes and squared her shoulders. Tomorrow would bring enslavement. If she wanted to escape, it had to be now.

From the shadows, she spied on Doc until he pulled himself from the pool, water sluicing from his nude body. Hazel averted her eyes, a blush staining her cheeks. She'd never seen a naked man before. Mentally slapping herself, she crept forward, her hand clenching the pipe as Doc wrapped a towel around his waist and bent to pick up his clothes.

Knock him on the back of his head. Just one swing.

He spun right as she swung.

"Haz—?" He never finished his word. His eyes rolled up into his head and she managed to grab his arm and shoulder before he could topple.

Pain struck her as she crashed to the ground, taking the brunt of his weight. Hazel wheezed as she wiggled out from underneath him and checked his pulse. It was steady. She snatched two towels from the basket and placed them underneath his head, then arranged his limbs in a more comfortable fashion.

A tear slipped from the corner of her eye as she stared down at Doc's face. "I'm so sorry," she choked out. "I wish there'd been another way."

Hazel turned from Doc and yanked the sheet from her knapsack. She ripped it in two and quickly tied knots in the sheet, then placed it on the edge before diving into the pool. Hazel scanned the rocks and plucked one from the bottom that was roughly the size of her fist. *That one should work.*

She heaved herself from the pool and tied the rock into the end of the sheet. Hazel snagged a soap bar and a hand towel and shoved them into her bag before throwing it over her chest. She glanced at Doc and then hopped into the water, the length of sheet trailing behind her. After paddling to almost the middle, she treaded water and eyed the wagon wheel above her. All she had to do was get the rock over one of the edges, then the rock would do the rest of the work.

Rotating the rock in her hand, she took a steady breath and then launched it, but missed it by three feet. Apparently, her aim wasn't as good as it used to be. Hazel towed the sheet back in and clutched the rock. She could do this. She tossed it again, and fear crawled up her throat as the rock smashed into the metal, the clang ringing through the room.

Oh, no. Desperately, she towed the sheet back in and eyed the entrance to the cave. Who knows who could have heard that. She needed to be out of there *now*. Her hand shook as she lifted the rock to toss it once more.

"You can do this," she whispered, taking a deep, even breath, her heart racing. "Calm down and focus."

Her papa's voice echoed through her mind. "Panic is your enemy. It'll kill you."

She steadied her hand, focused on the metal light, and threw the rock with all her might. Her heart skipped a beat as it sailed over the edge; she barely managed to snag the other end of the sheet. The other half of the sheet hung down, the rock swinging in the air as she swam closer.

Using one of the knots her brothers had taught her, she tied the two ends together. Hazel pulled them apart, threw one leg into the loop, and then the other, until she was sitting in the sheet like it was a giant swing. She jiggled a bit and a nervous giggle escaped her. The light stayed put. It wasn't going anywhere.

Slowly, she stood in the sheet and placed her hands on her makeshift rope. Gritting her teeth, she lifted her feet and wrapped her legs around the sheets. Her hands screamed and slipped a bit on the wet material, but she didn't fall. One foot at a time, she climbed until she reached the wagon wheel. Metal bit into her palms as she used the light to heave herself up. She wiggled and kicked until she lay flat on the wagon wheel, staring down at the pool.

Her stomach lurched. From up here, the light looked so much higher. Her arms shook as she pushed herself to her knees, balancing on the spokes, and hauled the sheet up after her. She couldn't leave a trail behind her. The Tainted had senses that she could only dream of.

Hazel unwrapped the rock and dropped it. It disappeared into the cloudy water with a dull plop. She glanced above and eyed the cables crisscrossing above her. A small grin tipped up her lips. How nice of them to make it an easy climb for her.

She tore four strips off the sheet and tied them around her palms and feet. Her hands and her feet were her most important assets for escape. Damaging them wasn't an option. She tore the ripped sheet in half and wrapped the other part around the spoke to hide it. It was too heavy to carry.

With her heart in her throat, she stood and reached for the first cable, not daring to look down. It was just like climbing trees. One by one, she climbed. Sweat ran down her temples; her breathing was labored as she reached for the last cable. She paused there, eyeing the last eight feet she had to climb. It wouldn't be easy, but she could do it.

Hazel pulled the sheet off her hands with her teeth

and placed a hand on each wall, then eased her feet out until they reached the wall, tension moving through her body.

"Only a little bit more to go, Haz," she murmured. "You climbed a tree with a dislocated shoulder and a broken arm. You've got this."

At said reminder, her wound complained. Hazel ignored it and began to climb, the rough sandstone tearing at her palms and the delicate skin of her feet.

The last eight feet seemed to take hours, but at last, her fingers curled over the rim. She hauled herself up and straddled the edge.

She'd made it. She'd *made* it!

She stifled the yell of triumph that threatened to spill from her lips and recovered from the climb. Relief swept through her at how the chute curved into a sedate slope instead of a sharp drop-off. Her breath caught as she moved her hair from her face and got a good look at her surroundings.

It wasn't a village. It was a massive compound.

The bluff was to the west just behind her, standing like a giant sentinel. The city spread out from there, some of the buildings built into the bluff. Farms edged the city like giant green rainbows, followed by two gigantic fences that looked like a jagged smile.

Her gaze moved toward the southern farms. That

was her way out.

She shimmied over the edge and carefully slid down the curl of the ceiling as quietly as she could while keeping an eye on her surroundings. Luck was on her side. The hot springs were on the edge of the compound.

The edge of the dome came quickly, and she winced as she realized she'd have to drop to the ground. It was far, but she wouldn't break her legs. Nevertheless, Hazel yanked the rest of her sheet from her bag and looped it around a jutting piece of rock. She eased over the side and began climbing down.

A ripping sound caught her attention right before she was airborne. Her scream stuck in her throat as she crashed to the ground. Blinding pain swamped her, but she couldn't cry. There wasn't any air. She frantically eyed the area around her through teary eyes and scooted herself into the shadows as she regained her breath.

Damn, that hurt ... but nothing is broken.

A small groan slipped from her as she pushed to her feet and glanced at the ripped sheet at her feet. Thank goodness it hadn't torn when she was inside. It had gotten her this far. She picked the sodden sheet from the ground and tucked it into her bag, then began moving through the shadows. Every sound made her cringe and look up.

That was many persons' mistake. They never looked up. But Hazel knew differently. Death came from above, and it had wings.

She froze and ducked behind a garbage can as two voices neared.

"Why aren't you home with that pretty wife of yours?" a male voice asked, his words slurred.

"She's mad at me," another male grumped, his voice growing closer.

"What did you do this time, Jo?"

"I forgot Molly."

The other man cackled, his laugh echoing around them. "How in the blazes did you forget your own daughter?"

The other man paused on the other side of the garbage and kicked at the dirt. Hazel held her breath and tried to blend into the brick wall at her back.

"Molly's so quiet. I thought she was following me." Hazel winced as the man kicked the garbage can. "It was an accident."

The other man cackled again and then began coughing. "God, that stinks. Like rotten eggs. What were the McDoogles eating today?" He slapped the other man on the back and led him away. "I'm sure if you grovel a little bit, she'll..." His voice trailed off as they disappeared around the corner.

Hazel let out the breath she was holding, yanked the sheet from her bag, and eyed the clothesline. She yanked a long, faded blue dress from the line and cut the bottom two feet off it. After tying a few knots, she had a new outfit and a new knapsack.

She shivered as she yanked her old dress off, replaced it with the new one, tossed the hot- spring-soaked sheet into the trash, arranged the garbage over the top of it, and then clipped her dress in place of the one she'd taken. Hopefully, that would cover what she'd taken. It was an even trade.

Weaving through the alleys and streets wasn't as difficult as it was confusing. It was a veritable maze. Her pulse picked up, though, when she finally reached the edge of the buildings and a sea of vegetables greeted her. She was so close.

She scoured the area for any sign of life and found none. This was the most dangerous part. If she could get to the vegetation, she'd be hidden, but there were thirty feet between her and the farm.

Hazel examined the area once more before bolting for the farm. Her heart hammered in her chest as she sprinted, bent low to the ground, dove between enormous tomato plants, and began army-crawling. She'd made it.

It was slow going, but in the end was worth it. First, a chain-link wall loomed ahead, topped with barbed wire. She paused and placed her cheek against the cool soil as exhaustion began to worm its way through her body. If she let herself, she could fall asleep right there.

"Get up," she whispered. "It's not that far. You can do this."

She pushed herself up and began to crawl again. Then, lights flooded the farm. Hazel didn't think, she just jumped to her feet and ran. Her arms pumped against her sides and she hit the fence in a full run. She scampered up the side and over the top, barely noticing the barbed wire cutting into her hands and then catching the inside of her thigh.

Once again, she hit the ground running. Shouts filled the air, but all she could hear was the pounding of her feet against the cracked earth. She could do this. Her legs quivered, but she forced herself to run faster. Whooshing filled her ears in time with her heartbeat, and time seemed to slow.

Twenty more feet.

Fifteen.

Ten.

Five.

She leapt for the fence and arms wrapped around

her waist. A scream exploded from her as the ground dropped from beneath her.

"No," she screamed, as they flew back over the fence, her escape shrinking into nothing with each beat of the monster's wings. "No!"

Hazel stumbled and fell to her knees as they touched the ground just outside the farm. Tears stung her eyes and sobs broke from her chest.

She'd been so close. Escape had been right there.

Hazel slammed her fist against the ground and yelled as more feet surrounded her.

"She almost made it. Unbelievable."

She glared at the monster to her left that was responsible for her capture. Brown feathered wings flared behind his back before he tucked them in. He gave her a rakish smile and winked at her.

"That was the most fun I've had all month."

"Piss off," she growled.

She skimmed over the crowd circling her. Three women with wicked-looking weapons, four with wings, and … her gaze stuttered over Clint, who stared at her with something akin to respect. She blinked. That wasn't right.

Feet slammed into the ground, the impact of a new arrival, and fear trickled through her veins like ice. The monster was there.

He stood from his crouch, looking like the devil himself. His gaze pinned her to the spot before he glanced at the brown-winged man. "Jameson, report."

"It was a fluke that I caught her. I almost didn't catch her movement. She was creeping through the farm. She made it over the first fence and almost the second."

She glanced at the ground, more tears flooding her eyes. *Almost.* What an ugly, disappointing word.

Her skin prickled as she knew the monster was staring at her. She glared at her bloody hands. There was no way in hell she'd cower at his feet.

Despite her fear, fatigue, and pain, she pulled herself up to her feet, swaying. Jameson reached for her, but she ripped her blade from the sheath she'd made for her thigh. "Don't touch me."

Jameson held his hands up and took a step back. "I was only trying to help."

She turned toward the monster, who looked like he was about to explode, and pointed her dagger at him, ignoring the Tainted that now surrounded her like vultures. "Let me go."

His midnight eyes narrowed on the blade. "You shouldn't point that at someone unless you know how to use it."

"Come a little closer and I'll show you a few things,"

she said with a slight purr. If he came any closer, she'd cut his black heart from his chest.

He laughed, the sound mocking and scornful.

"Son," Clint said softly, and placed a scaled hand on the monster's shoulder. "I wouldn't taunt her. Take a deep breath."

The world blurred a little bit and rolled, but Hazel managed to keep her feet. She'd overdone it.

The monster inhaled deeply and then stilled. She swallowed a bit, unnerved at his statue impression. The world rolled again as her pain began to filter back in. Her hands burned, and her thigh throbbed with the beat of her heart. She stumbled again, accidentally grabbing Jameson's wing. Hazel recoiled and fell to one knee.

Hands seized her arms and she struggled to get away. "Don't touch me! Don't touch me!"

"Stop it," the monster growled, shaking her a little. "You're hurt."

Hazel fought harder and stabbed at his side. He hissed out a breath. "Dad."

Clint snagged her blade from her hand, and she screamed, snapping her teeth in his direction. "You're a liar."

He frowned at her as he pocketed her blade and stared at her with concern. "You need to let him check you."

"Like hell," she screeched.

The monster immobilized her arms and locked her against his chest. His other hand wandered down to the hem of her dress and yanked it up.

"Stop touching me," she yelled, her voice breaking with sobs.

"I'm not going to hurt you," he yelled back.

She cried out as he touched whatever hurt on her thigh. Hazel crashed her head forward, pain pounding through her head. She bared her teeth at him when his nose began to bleed. That bastard deserved to bleed, to hurt as bad as she did. The world spun once more, and then the monsters surrounded her.

Hazel closed her eyes, fighting off the nausea and the fear.

"Hazel?"

She pried one eye open at the familiar voice and almost wept. "Doc, I'm sorry. Please don't let him hurt me." It killed her to beg, but she'd do just about anything to get out of the monster's arms.

His amber gaze slid to the monster. "She needs care and is losing blood. Give her to me."

Her eyes drooped, and her head tipped onto the monster's shoulder. She tried to move it, but her head was just too heavy. "I hate you," she whispered.

"I know," the monster said softly. "I won't hurt you. I promise."

She puffed out a laugh with the last of her energy. "You already have."

To be continued in The Exiled: Dominion of Ash Book Two

ABOUT THE AUTHOR

Bestselling Author Frost Kay is a certified book dragon with an excessive TBR, and a shoe obsession. If you love bewitching fantasy and sci-fi, epic adventures, dark promises, thrilling action, swoon worthy anti heroes, and slow burning romance; her books are for you!

Fans of Frost Kay love her epic and science fiction teen titles for their "witty banter and exquisitely crafted sentences (that) never leave you bored or wanting," and "find the writing on par with Queen (Sarah J.) Maas and Elise Kova."

You can find her at www.frostkay.net

Frost Kay is the author of three series:

The Aermian Feuds

1- Rebel's Blade

2 - Crown's Shield

2.5 - Siren's Lure

3 - Enemy's Queen

4 - King's Warrior

5 - Spy's Mask (summer 2019)

6 - Court's Fool (winter 2019)

Mixologists and Pirates

1 - Amber Vial

2 - Emerald Bane

3 - Scarlet Venom

4 - Cyan Toxin

5 - Onyx Elixir

6 - Indigo Alloy (Summer 2019)

The Dominion of Ash

0.5 - The Strain

1 - The Tainted

2 - The Exiled (fall 2019)

Made in the USA
Columbia, SC
11 August 2020

15999923R00174